Night Briars

by Taryn Tyler

For Zachary Hernandez

Thank you to my patrons Kimberly ad JJ Elliot for helping supply the coffee needed to write this book. Your support means everything to me.

ACKNOWLEDGMENTS

No human is an island and no creative endeavor is accomplished alone. Thank you to my sister, Shay Tyler, for reading so many fairytales with me in our high school years. Thank you to my mom, Debra Tyler, for allowing me to write as homework when I first discovered my passion for it. Also to my college writing teachers Gary Philips and Lisa Shapiro for helping me hone and embrace my talent. I never would have believed in my work without your enthusiastic encouragement. And of course, thank you to all my wonderful critique partners who provided valuable feedback as I plugged my way through draft after draft. Whitney Coleman Brandenburg, Courtney Longshore, JJ Elliot, Hali Tyler, L.T. Host, and Kerrian Martin. You guys rock!.

Sing me a Lullaby

Sing me a lullaby
Sing me a song
Sing me a lullaby
Before you are gone
Sing to me please,
I am afraid
Sing to me comfort
So I can be brave
Sing me a lullaby
Sing me a song
Sing me a lullaby
Before you are gone

Your voice is soothing
Drone close to my ear
Hum any melody
Let me know you are near
Sing me a lullaby
Sing me a song
Sing me a lullaby
Before you are gone

Sing to me now
Our fate is unknown
Sing to me softly
Remind me of home
Sing me a lullaby
Sing me a song
Sing me a lullaby
Before you are gone

SNOW

I woke in the night. The cottage air was warm and crisp. Open like the black air outside or a deep sleep, void of dreams. Rose lay beside me, her long lashes closed over the tops of sharp cheekbones. A wash of moonlight poured in from the window, painting her delicate nose and gently curved smile a pale, silvery white. She snored softly as she slept.

My arm cramped beneath her shoulder. I shifted it, releasing the pressure. I pressed my palm against the warmth of her neck with my other hand, smoothing the red curls away from her face.

Rose jerked away from my touch. She gasped in her sleep. Her legs struggled to untangle themselves from mine.

I pulled my hand away and unwound myself from her.

It was her dreams she shrank from. Her memories of him, not me. I reminded myself of this but the hurt still stung as if I were the monster she feared.

I watched her flail back and forth in our loft as the dream persisted. If I woke her she would only be more likely to remember it in the light of day. I edged myself even further from her in the hay. I could not go with her into her dreams. I could not be there to tell her that she was safe. That I would not let anyone hurt her ever again.

My arms and legs tensed. It was too difficult to sleep without the warm press of her body against mine. I rolled out from underneath the quilt and clattered down out of the loft. The ladder only creaked a little. My feet didn't make a sound as I made my way across the cottage floor, opened the door, and stepped outside.

The stars were bright, sprinkled like ashes across the rich night sky. I could feel them wrap around me like the embrace I longed for.

When Rose had had her magic --before she used it all up to break herself out of Lucille's curse --had the stars sung to her? She had never said so. She had said that the forest had. Our garden had. The red and white roses that wove their way over the cottage walls, intertwining around each other as our love intertwined us had. She has said that the animals had sung to her. But she had never mentioned the stars.

Standing solid on the ground, looking up at the sky, I felt as if the stars could sing if they wanted to. As if they were a choir and sky were their cathedral.

I had never been to a cathedral of course but Papa had. He had said that they had great big halls with windows made of colored glass and the people in them sang.

The door clicked behind me. I turned.

Rose poked her head out. She yawned. She pulled the quilt tight around her shoulders even though it wasn't cold. Her lips bent into a pout. "You left me."

"You were having a nightmare." I said.

She paused. Her eyes grew distant as if trying to remember something then she blinked, flicking the remnants of the dreams away. She stepped outside and flung the quilt around my shoulders. "I used to hold you when you had nightmares. Not get up and walk away."

I stepped closer, nestling my breasts against the soft curves of hers. I placed my hands around the back of her neck, meeting her gaze. "You pushed me away."

Rose looked down. The distant look returned to her eyes but only for a moment. "I'm sorry, Snow." She kissed me gently on the lips. She tasted like summer. Like warm milk on a cold night. "You know it's not you I'm pushing away."

"I know." I said. "I'd kill him again if I could. He can't hurt you anymore, Rose."

She looked down again. The moonlight gleamed against her lashes. "If only it worked that way."

I could almost feel the memories manifest in her mind. Him dragging her up to his chamber inside the manor. Her unable to move as he unlaced her bodice and pulled up her skirt. My blood boiled at the thought. I instinctively reached for my knife although, of course, I wasn't wearing it. Instead, I grabbed a fist full of my night shift.

Rose saw the motion. She laughed. Her nose scrunched and she snorted. Softly. Like a log crackling with fire. She turned me around so that I could lean back against her as we both faced the woodlands. The moss glow of dawn traced the tops of the trees almost as if the light came from the forest itself. Rose held me tight around the middle. She nuzzled her nose against the back of my head. "The sun is coming up."

The stars vanished one by one, fading like raindrops at the touch of the sun. The jade glow around the trees brightened into a pale liquid gold framed with pink and violet hues reaching all the way across the sky. The slow, tiny heart of time pulsed by one thump at a time until the vibrant garden of colors melted out of the sky, leaving only the soft, ordinary whisper of morning.

Something stirred in the trees.

"First-Light." Rose's breath tickled against my neck, startling me out of my almost slumber. "It's time for his berries."

A deer poked his long narrow nose out of the forest. Four long willowing legs and little black hooves followed. The deer twitched his nose. He stared at Rose with big black eyes.

First-Light. Rose had ripped his mother's heart out when he was a fawn to fool Lucille into thinking Rose was dead. She had raised him to make up for it as best she could. Full grown now, he could forage for himself but he still came every morning, expecting to eat from her hand.

Most days she obliged.

I sighed, reluctant to pull myself away from Rose's embrace. "If he's ready for his breakfast I had better go inside and prepare ours."

Rose tensed. Her arm tightened around my waist. She kissed me lightly against the cheek. "Get some rest. I'll make breakfast."

I turned to face her with raised eyebrows. "My cooking isn't as bad as all that."

She opened and closed her lashes softly. "Snow, yesterday you put pine nuts and lavender in the oatcakes. With no honey. They tasted like dry bits of earth you had picked up off the forest floor for us to eat."

"We were out of honey." I protested.

"Because you put it in our pea soup last week."

I winced. That particular undertaking had been an undeniable failure. I opened my mouth to protest that I could make plain ordinary porridge sweetened with berries if that's what she wanted but it didn't sound like very much fun. Rose was much better at ordinary food than I was.

Rose saw the concession in my eyes. She kissed my nose. "We'll go to the hives today for some honey. Then you can weave together whatever ingredients your heart desires."

It was a perfect day for a walk. Warm but not hot with a light, crisp breeze that tangled into the roots of our hair as we crunched our feet against the autumn leaves. Rose walked in long, careless strides as if there was nothing in the world that wasn't her friend. As if she knew for certain that she belonged wherever she happened to be standing. Her long, red cloak rippled around her boots, billowing in the breeze with each step. I stumbled along beside her, scurrying like a squirrel on my shorter legs with a satchel over one arm and a bundle of firewood beneath the other.

First-Light drifted in and out of the bushes sometimes up ahead of us and sometimes a ways behind. I had learned to recognize the distinctive fall of his hooves and wave of his tail. I had to when I went hunting for venison. Rose would never forgive me if I accidently brought him home for dinner.

I would never forgive myself.

Pools of light poured in through the canopy of oak leaves, trickling in thick, warm waves against our skin. Rose stopped suddenly. The bucket of water in her hands splashed over the side, soaking into the woodland floor.

"That's Gran's song." She turned toward me.

I stopped beside her. I hadn't realized I had been humming. I smiled at her. "I must have learned it from you."

She nodded distractedly. It was her Gran's songs that had taught her her magic. She'd been lulled to sleep by them in the cradle and they had taught her to listen to the music of the forest and spark fires into being with her eyes.

"Do you miss being a witch?" I asked.

She shook her head. Her curls shifted like soft petals around her ears. Her nose wrinkled as her smile spread over her face once more, bright and sprightly. "Do you miss being a princess?"

"No." I grinned. Most days I forgot I had ever been one. The long dreary days in Papa's manor eating court dinners and being polite to Lucille seemed like a lifetime ago. It was nothing like the freedom of being here in the woods with Rose. "The only thing I miss from the manor is Papa."

And the books. But Otto had sent some of them to me when I had pledged my birthright to him. I kept them in the chest beneath the loft.

"You were a princess too." I reminded her. She still was a princess actually. Otto was her brother and he ruled both Papa's manor and the great castle in the north.

She shook her head. "I was a baby. I don't even remember."

Rose touched the clasp on her cloak just beneath her throat. Her Gran had made it for her. Except that her Gran hadn't really been her Gran at all. Just her nurse who had cared for her in her parents' castle.

She pulled her hand away. She set the bucket of water on the ground and reached into her pocket, pulling out a glint. She wrinkled her nose. "I bet you wish I was still a witch. We wouldn't need this."

It was true. Once she had been able to light fires with her eyes. Now we needed a flint.

I handed her two sticks from the bundle of firewood under my arm. Rose struck the stones against each other until they created a spark then held them over the wood. They caught fire then faded to a soft smoulder, streaming a steady burn of smoke into the air. She handed one stick to me. The smoke filtered into my eyes and nostrils. I squinted then sneezed.

If she still had her magic we wouldn't need smoke at all. Her song would have been enough to lull the bees away from their honey.

Her smile flickered, brightening into the burn in her eyes as she met my gaze. "I can do the climbing this time."

My heart burst inside my breast. She might need a flint to smoke out bees but she could still ignite every bit of my being with that smile. I shook my head, feeling the glow in my own eyes as I returned her gaze. "I'll climb." I said. I was smaller and more nimble from hunting.

We held the smoking sticks as we walked. It wasn't long before we heard the hive. A sharp, inconsistent susurration wafted into our ears, growing louder and louder. Soon we began to see small scatterings of bees hovering over yarrow and goldenrod blossoms on the woodland floor. We kept the smoking sticks in front of us. Bees drifted away from the pale grey wafts of smoke streaming from the embers, creating a path for us. The smoke confused the bees. They weren't likely to sting us until we were near their queen but we didn't want the gatherers here on the fringe of the hive to alert the others of our approach.

The coarse drone of their song grew louder and louder until the sound was almost deafening. We twisted our way around one tree and then another. Suddenly we were standing at the bottom of the oak where the hive was nested.

I stared up at the thick cluster of bees swarming over the bright golden honeycomb. The bees were so close together that they almost looked like one giant insect hovering near the top of the tree. It was a tall oak. The knot where the honey was lodged hung at least four times my height into the air.

Rose pulled out her flint again. I handed her the rest of the firewood then helped her clear the leaves as she arranged the wood beneath the hive.

It took awhile for the flames to catch this time. The crisp autumn breeze had grown stronger. At last the fire flickered over the firewood, crackling lightly at first, then roaring into a heavy burst of orange and blue and gold. Rose and I stepped back. Warmth flushed over my nose and ears. Smoke seeped into my nose and throat. I sneezed. The thick, white-gray fog climbed up the trunk of the oak, reaching its misty fingers around the branches and up into the hive. The buzzing den drifted down to a soft, dull hum as I stooped to unlace my boots.

Rose looked at me from across the fire. Her face was red from the heat. She grinned. "Good luck."

I peeled my boots off and shouldered my satchel over my arm, feeling the weight of my knife and jar inside. I placed my smoke stick carefully inside with the smoking point poking out.

Still on her knees, Rose clasped her hands together and held them out for me. I placed my foot into her palms and she hoisted me up onto the trunk of the oak.

The ascent was slow. The bark scratched my hands and feet despite my callouses. I had to press my knees around the trunk and pull myself up with my arms until I reached the first branch. Bees swarmed around my face, lulled but not stopped by the seductive lilt of the smoke. My eyes began to water. I held back a cough, not wanting to disturb them any more than I had to.

I reached the first branch and grasped my hands around it, pulling myself up. My shoulders were strong from cutting wood. I lifted my hips and middle with ease and placed my feet onto the branch.

A piercing bite jabbed into the bottom of my foot. I bit my lip, holding back a cry, and bent to remove the stinger. Standing on one foot, I leaned my hips back and my chest forward to keep my balance. A bee landed on my shoulder. Another landed on my nose.

I placed my foot down -still sore and screaming with venom -careful not to step on a bee again. I pulled the smoke stick out of my satchel and waved it near my face. The bees cleared, drifting away from the smoke. They thinned near my line of vision so that I could see the next branch more clearly.

I placed the stick back in the satchel. The next branch wasn't too much higher up. If I stood on the tips of my toes and twisted my spine just so . . .

There. My hands gripped over the rough, bark covered surface. I pulled myself up slowly then swung my knees up through my arms and lowered them down onto the branch, careful not to crush another bee beneath the folds of my skirt.

I was an arm's length from the hive now. Bees swarmed in every direction around me. I hung back. Too many quick movements this close to the queen and I would be swollen from head to toe. I pulled the stick out once again and held it out in front of me. My movements were painfully slow and precise as I pulled the jar from my satchel, unplugged the cork, and lodged the jar between my knees. Time moved like the slow drip of honey, each second sticking to the next. Bees buzzed around my ears and eyes and neck, landing in my hair and on my shoulders and toes and fingers. I tightened my thighs around the jar to hold it in place and pulled my knife out of the satchel.

I reached my arm out with the smoke stick in front of me and inch by tiny inch moved toward the hive.

The gold of the honeycomb was bright and vibrant. It was a small hive. When we had first found it I had hoped it would grow enough so that we could sell the extra honey in the village. Rose had said that it was just as well that it didn't. The villagers were likely to come looking for the hive themselves if they knew it was here and it was important to leave enough honey to get the bees through the winter or there wouldn't be any at all come spring.

I sometimes forgot that the villagers were no longer afraid of the woods. Not since Rose and I had convinced them that the ghosts and weres had left when Lucille had.

My knife's blade touched the comb. The edge was sharp. I held it back with control to make the slice slow, still holding the smoke out in front of me. The bees swarmed around me in a confused dance. A sting cut into the back of my ear.

A wince jumped up into my body but I held it back. I kept my hands steady. Smooth, thick honey coated my fingers as I lifted the slice of comb just as slowly as I had sliced it and slid it into the jar.

The jar held three more slices. Securing them was a slow and laborious process. I was stung twice more and pricked my finger with the knife edge. Deep, red blood dripped onto the oak bark and my finger throbbed but I kept working.

At last I placed my knife --gold and gooey with honey --back into the satchel and shoved the stopper into the jar with my sticky, honey covered hands. Four slices of comb gleamed through the glass. Any more and the bees wouldn't last the winter. We could survive without honey but the forest needed the bees. I placed the jar in the satchel along with the knife and the smoke stick and made my way back towards Rose.

Going down was quicker than coming up. I used my weight to drop from one branch to the next --checking first to make sure I didn't land on any bees -- then dropped straight down onto the ground. The buzzing up above grew louder. The hive was coming out of their daze, realizing that some of their comb was gone.

I landed feet first on a coarse, crinkly covering of oak leaves. I heard a soft sizzling sound beside me and turned to see Rose pouring her bucket of water onto the flames. She tossed my boots into the empty bucket and grabbed my hand. We darted into the woods, putting as much distance between us and the wakening bees as we could.

We slowed our pace as we reached the stream and stopped. I knelt to wash the sticky honey off my knife and fingers. Rose dug the bee stingers out of my foot and ear and hand. She applied a salve to the tender skin then kissed the sting behind my ear. Her tongue crawled playfully into the inside of my ear folds. I giggled and lifted my still sticky fingers for her to suck clean.

"So sweet." She cooed, moving her lips up my fingers to my hand. She kissed her way up my arm and neck. I leaned forward, meeting her lips with mine as they reached my face. Our tongues intertwined like the rose vines outside our house. Her kiss was warm and familiar. I sank into the taste of it, losing myself in every nuance of flavor.

We sat back against a tree, listening to the water in the stream. I leaned my head against her breasts. My eyelids grew heavy like stones. I let them fall deeper and deeper, dripping slowly into oblivion.

"Snow." Rose's touch pulled me awake. I opened my eyes with a gasp, pulling away from her touch.

Rose leaned back. Her eyes narrowed in concern. "Now who's having nightmares?"

"Just a deep sleep." The words didn't taste quite true. I searched through my mind for the memory of what my dreams had been but there was nothing there but a gaping hole. Blackness.

Rose opened her mouth then closed it. I couldn't tell if she believed me or not. "It's getting dark." She said "Let's go home."

Dusk rustled through the woodland. A fox stirred not far from us. An owl hooted in the distance. Rose suggested lighting a torch to see by but it would take time to light. If we hurried we could reach the cottage before full night fell. It grew cold as we walked. Rose draped part of her cloak over my shoulders, sharing its warmth with me.

We saw the bridge before we saw the cottage. The trees around us thinned and there was the shadow of three planks stretched over the stream in the almost dark. A pathway leading us home. My stomach gurgled. I wasn't sure I would have the patience to cook tonight after all. Perhaps we would heat yesterday's pea soup and save the honey for tomorrow. The water trickled by in a soft, insistent whisper as we neared the bridge.

Something else was near the bridge. Another shadow, this one less familiar. It leaned against a tree. I stared, trying to riddle out what it was.

He straightened when he saw us.

Rose and I stopped. We turned to face each other. Her eyes were narrowed in the dim light.

"Trouble." She muttered.

We quickened our pace. I let the cloak fall away from my shoulders as I pushed forward, struggling to keep up with Rose's long strides.

The shadow stepped onto the bridge as we reached it. He faced us directly, reaching only to Rose's knees. Up close we could see his long beard and gold threaded coat. He pointed a tiny, boney finger at us.

"Well." His voice was tight and scratchy like tree bark. "What kind of welcome do you call that? Leaving a fellow out in the cold while you great milk sopped things lollygag in the forest, getting up to who knows what. I'm frozen solid through thanks to the pair of you!"

"Trouble!" I stooped low and closed my arms around the little hobgoblin. The embrace was as gentle as I could manage so as not to crush his tiny bones. I pulled back, grinning. "What are you doing this far south? I thought you were part of Otto's court now."

Trouble cleared his throat. He brushed off his coat. "You've wrinkled the silk." He said but even in the dusk I could see traces of a blush in the corners of his face that weren't covered by his beard. "After I've come all this way to see you. Well." He crossed his arms. "What have you two got to say for yourselves?"

Rose shrugged. "We were gathering honey. It's not as if you had sent word that you were coming."

"Ha!" was his only reply. He scowled.

I laughed. "We're glad to see you Trouble. Come inside and get warm. We'll make you some seared rabbit and onions." I had to make a fresh supper now. We so seldom had visitors. Fortunately we had some salted rabbit that was still fresh. It wouldn't take long to sear and season.

"Rabbit and onion." Rose said. "You aren't going to put the honey in that are you?"

I turned toward her and brushed my fingers against the soft curve of her chin. I tilted my head and let my eyelashes drop and lift over my eyes. "You said I could make whatever I wanted."

"Yes, but--"

I kissed her nose. "Trust me."

I turned toward the cottage. Rose and Trouble followed me over the bridge and across the clearing. They waited as I unlatched the door and held it open for them then we all stepped inside.

Rose lit the fire. Trouble scrutinized her closely as she knelt next to the stove with the flint. I located the salted rabbit meat, garlic, and onions and set to work putting it all together. Rose cast me a suspicious glance as I poured on the honey. I grinned at her. She turned toward Trouble as he rubbed his long fingered hands next to the fire.

"What are you doing here?" Rose asked him. "You've come a long way for rabbit and onions with honey."

Trouble narrowed his eyes. "A gentleman deals with business after supper is over."

Rose placed her hands on her hip. She raised her eyebrows. "I am not a gentleman."

"Ha!" The delicate embroidery of Trouble's gold coat flickered in the firelight. He reached into the inside pocket and pulled out a small roll of paper sealed with wax. "For you, Red Witch." He held it out to her, palm upward, bowing his head in a rare show of supplication.

Rose snatched it out of his hand. "I'm not a witch anymore."

"A witch isn't something you can stop being." He said.

Rose stared at the letter in her hand. The red wax seal had the same rose carving as the clasp on her cloak. "It's from Otto."

It wasn't really a question but Trouble nodded anyways.

Rose held the letter in her hand, staring at the seal as if it might sink its teeth into her.

ROSE

I touched the clasp at my neck. Gran's clasp she had made me. She had told me that the rose engraved on it was to represent my name but she hadn't told me that it was also my family's crest. Seeing the same rose on the wax seal in my hand felt like a violation. As if Otto had stolen something from me. Something that had been mine and Gran's but now was his too along with centuries of dead nobles who had nothing to do with me.

"We can wait until after supper." Trouble sniffed pointedly at the air, glancing over at the rabbit and onions as it began to sizzle over the fire.

Snow looked up from stirring the meat with a wooden spoon. Her intense, dark eyes drifted out of the glazed, concentrated look they held when she was cooking. She smiled at me. Her sweet, trusting smile. She could melt iron with it if she wanted to. "It's only a letter, Rose. It's not going to bite you."

I returned the smile with a weak upward tilt of my lips then stared back at the letter. What could be so important that the king of the north was sending me a message about it? What did he want from me?

The king of the north. My brother. Otto. Our red bear.

It was different for Snow. She had been raised in the splendor of her papa's manor house. She was accustomed to the ways of kings. But I had been raised in the village by Greta and Gran, never knowing that nobles had anything to do with me until Otto had come along, telling me he was my brother. I had liked him better as a bear before Trouble had broken the curse Lucille had put on him.

I split open the seal and unrolled the paper. The message was short and to the point. Perhaps because Otto knew that I wasn't as fond of reading as Snow was.

"Well?" Snow poked her spoon at the onions as they began to brown. I could smell the sweetness from the honey filling the cottage. "What does Otto say?"

I looked up from the message. "He's getting married. He wants us to go to the wedding."

"Oh!" There was laughter in Snow's voice. Her eyes glistened like icicles in the firelight. She was positively giddy. "It will be wonderful to see him again."

I opened my mouth. A king's wedding? That meant balls and parades and long, lavish dinners. I pulled my cloak over the front of my plain wool bodice without meaning to, remembering the tattered velvet gown Snow had been wearing when she had first stepped into this cottage so many years ago. How could I tell her that I would rather dance on hot coals than go to my own brothers wedding?

I didn't have to tell her. She read it in my eyes. Her smile melted away. She turned toward Trouble as he watched us with his arms crossed next to the fire. "It would be a long journey." She said. "We can't be away from the cottage for so long. It might be overrun with mice or stolen by a villager or _"

"Greta can check in on the cottage while we're gone." I said.

Snow snapped her head around to look at me, puzzled.

I smiled. I wasn't going to deny her the journey simply because I didn't like castles. Besides. Otto was my brother. He had spent a whole spring and summer with us inside this very cottage and every winter before that when he had still been a bear.

"I wouldn't worry too much about the cottage." Trouble said. "It's not much worth protecting."

I glanced around the cottage. There was a leak in the roof that needed to be repaired. The glass in one of our windows was cracked. Our furniture was limited to a table, two chairs, the fireplace, Gran's old wardrobe, and a stool with a wobbly leg. With the rickety old ladder leading up into the loft and the pots and dried garlic hanging from the ceiling it was a cramped space. Nothing like the spacious halls of Snow's papa's manor house.

Still. This cottage was home. It was a place that belonged to us and no one else.

I turned and glared at him. "Just because you've grown fat at a king's table wearing silk shirts. Do I need to remind you that you and your brothers used to live in a hovel?"

"Ha!" He sat down on the stool, glaring. "It was a very large hovel. With a treasure trove."

Snow's rabbit and onions was glorious. Sweet from the honey. Rich and savory from the onions. She served it with soft bread and butter and a dark woodland tea. Her successful concoctions never ceased to amaze me. They almost made up for the disasters she made. Trouble hardly looked up from his bowl as he devoured three helpings. It was a wonder so much food could fit in such a tiny little body. When he had finished he told us about his journey from the north.

"Otto wanted to send an entire entourage." He said. "Pompous oaf! An army sized escort would have taken months to get through that narrow pass. It's as narrow as a courtier's mind."

I watched Trouble as he leaned back next to the fire, looking for a pipe inside his gold waistcoat pocket. He loved the splendor I had no doubt. Hobgoblins were like magpies the way they collected sparkling objects. And yet he seemed so comfortable in the rugged atmosphere of our cottage despite his criticism of it. Perhaps the narrow pass wasn't the only reason he had insisted on fetching us on his own. Perhaps he hadn't warmed to the formalities of the castle as much as he would have us believe.

"I've never seen mountains up close before." Snow said. There was that giddy look in eyes again. The laughter in her voice. She was preening with eagerness.

Trouble pulled his pipe out of his pocket and stooped to light it in the fire. "They're a lot like the plains except they're easier to fall off of."

I went to see Greta the next morning. I reached the village a little after dawn. The autumn fog thickened the air. A damp chill seeped through my cloak. It was worn now, not bright and vibrant as it had been when Gran had given it to me what seemed like a lifetime ago. The scents of yeast and melted iron wafted through the village streets. I could hear the dull, insistent clamour of the blacksmith purifying his ore from inside his forge. It was barely after dawn but villagers seldom wasted daylight.

Greta was standing outside her door when I reached it. She had a basket of fresh bread swung over her arm and a pail of milk in her hand. She was a plain woman with small lips and narrow eyes but she grinned when she saw me. Her whole face lit up like a harvest bonfire, crackling with beauty. I waved, happy to see her. Her smile faded as I got closer.

"You look worried." She said.

"I am."

She opened her door and I followed her inside.

"Sit down." Greta gestured toward her table and chair next to her spinning wheel. She pulled two wooden mugs out of her cupboard and filled them with the fresh, warm milk from her pail. The liquid echoed inside the wooden mugs as she poured. She sat in the chair across from me, reaching for her spinning. Greta more than any of the other villagers never wasted daylight. The familiar whir of the wheel sent me back to the early years of my life when the world was simple with no kings or witches or hobgoblins.

And no Snow.

There had only been me and Greta and sometimes Gran and the constant whir of the spinning wheel. My hands danced for a moment, involuntarily mimicking Greta's hand as she worked. It was tempting to wish my life was still that simple but I had hated the dullness of it. I wouldn't have survived it at all if it hadn't been for Gran's laughter and the songs she sang. If it hadn't been for the wrinkles in her eyes when she smiled.

It was her songs that had taught me to be a witch.

"What's the trouble, Rose?" Greta asked. She looked up from her work as she spoke but her hands never paused in their dance.

"Not trouble." I said. "Well, Trouble is here but that's just the hobgoblin's name. Snow and I are traveling north for the king's wedding."

Greta raised an eyebrow. "The king is getting married?"

I nodded.

"That's a long way to travel for a wedding."

I nodded again. She had known that I was a princess from the north when she had agreed to raise me, long before I had known myself. Sometimes it felt as if the whole world had conspired to keep the truth from me. "Will you check in on our cottage while we are away?" I asked. "Make sure it is not overrun?"

Greta nodded. "Of course.'

"Thank you."

The hum of the spinning wheel buzzed on, filling the space of the house. I looked down at the untouched milk in front of me. The white liquid looked almost gray in the shadows cast by the walls.

"You don't want to go."

I looked up, surprised. "It will be a long journey." I said. "We won't be able to come home until spring."

She stared at me. Serene. Almost eerie. She could see that there was more. I almost felt that she could read my thoughts. That she knew just by looking at me that I was worried Otto would ask Snow to marry him again despite his betrothal to a southern princess. That the splendor of his castle would entice her away from me. That I wondered what right I had ever had to keep her away from the birthright of her royalty in the first place.

"I've never been to a castle before." Was all I said.

"You were born in one." She reminded me. "You were born in that one."

"I was a baby. I don't remember any of it. I don't know how to dance or hunt or eat court dinners."

"You chew them." Greta said.

I could have made her my handmaid I realized. If I'd gone with Otto the first time he'd asked me to. When he'd asked me to live at the castle with him and rule by his side. Would she have liked that? To be taken away from this drab little village to live with courtiers and wear fine clothes? I tried to imagine her in silk but couldn't quite manage it. She would laugh at such finery.

My eyes moved back to her hands, dancing over the wool she spun as we spoke. She was using a new spindle carved with leaves running like a vine from the tip. My eyebrows arched, surprised to see something so unpractical in her possession.

"That's pretty." I said.

Greta blushed. Like her smile, it made her features burst with beauty. "Bert made it for me."

I grinned. Bert, the village carpenter, had been here the last time I'd come to visit Greta. He'd been repairing her roof but I had suspected he'd had something else in mind from the way he'd been casting eyes at her. I was glad to hear that I was right.

"I'll be going to your wedding next." I said.

She shook her head. Her blush deepened. "At my age? Not likely."

"You'll be married by spring. I stake my life on it."

She stopped spinning. Silence struck the house so suddenly that it felt almost as if my ears had been slapped. She looked at me, deep and serious.

I squirmed in my seatt as if I were a child again, afraid to be scolded.

"Snow chose you." She said. "She chose to give up her birthright just as you chose to give up yours. You chose each other. You have nothing to fear."

But I did fear. Despite all the love and devotion Snow had shown me I feared that a castle might show her how unworthy of her I really was.

Snow had everything packed when I returned to the cottage. We didn't need to bring much. A sack of turnips, the rest of the salted rabbit, a couple of flints, Snow's traps and skinning knives, her mother's silver jewelry, and Gran's journal. I carried the turnips and salted rabbit. She carried everything else.

"Best to head out now." Trouble said. "We can still gain a few leagues before dusk. The mountain passages will be impossible once the snow sets in and it's going to be an early winter."

We stood outside the cottage door. I slung the pack of turnips and rabbit over my shoulder. Our red and white roses tumbled up and down the outer walls, gripping the stone like a child grips its mother. The shed behind the cottage was still, almost covered in shadows from the trees. I turned my neck, twisting to see behind me. The fence we had never bothered to repair stretched out over the glade, out to the bridge, leading the way to the woodland that still felt like more a part of me than my own skin even long after I had stopped hearing it sing to me. My hand lingered over the cottage latch. I held the coarse texture of the wood captive beneath my fingers.

A gentle touch lifted my wrist and pulled my hand away from the wood. The latch fell. The thump echoed through the stillness of the wood like a cry for help.

Snow pulled the red curls away from my face with a soft caress. She kissed my cheek. "It will still be here when we get back, Rose."

I looked down at her. Her gaze was deep and enticing. Black like the night sky. "It will be different." I said. "We will be different."

Snow ran her thumb up and down my ear. Her touch was soft. Comforting. Familiar. "We would become different if we stayed too. Time does that, not places."

She was right. I knew she was. But it was still hard to leave the place I had always been the happiest. A whole winter was such a long time to be gone.

"Will you great big milk sops hurry up?" Trouble shouted from the edge of the bridge. "At this rate it'll be spring before our feet touch the road."

We turned and caught up with him at the edge of the bridge. It was a pleasant trek, though tiring as late morning wore into afternoon. We wound our way through the still canopy of the trees, lulled by the rustling of the wind and the occasional rabbit bounding through the bushes.

Snow chattered, twittering like a bird about the fall of the sunlight through the leaves and the distance of the rabbits, how difficult it would be to catch one in her traps in the autumn when the stores of the forest were plentiful and there was little that could entice them into her grasp.

"But there's more game in the autumn than in the winter" She said "so even though they're harder to catch it's still easier to hunt."

Trouble tramped up ahead, leading the way just out of earshot.

Snow grew quiet as we neared the manor house where she had grown up. The place she had learned to keep secrets. Where Lucille had poisoned her father.

The thick stone walls loomed into view. The gate beneath the guard house was lowered so that we could see the keep and ward inside. We had both been held captive in those towers before. Snow as a girl, struck with grief and smothered in dangerous secrets, and me . . .

But that didn't matter anymore. Lucille and Boris were dead. Otto had appointed a warden of his own choosing to look after the manor and the villages thrived under his rule.

Snow's eyes lingered over the building as we passed it, silent, respectful almost. At last she turned toward me. Her head tilted in contemplation. "Do you think Otto will love his bride?" She asked.

I shrugged, trying to hide the discomfort that her interest in Otto's bride gave me. "I thought you said nobles never married for love."

"They don't. They marry for land and heirs and necessary alliances but . . ." Her forehead wrinkled. "Perhaps they still can love each other. After they are married. Papa seldom spoke of my mother except to say that she was good at needlepoint but there was a fondness when he spoke. Respect, I think. If she had not died so soon he might have grown to love her."

"But would she have loved him?" I asked.

Snow bit her lip. This was a piece of her past she would never find answers for.

"She was from the Southern Ridges wasn't she, your mother?"

We both looked down, surprised to see Trouble slowing downs to fall into pace with us.

"Yes." Snow said. "Elise and Dana came with her when she and Papa married. They were her handmaidens before they were mine. They said that the snow fascinated her because she had never seen any in the South. They told me she wished for a daughter the first night she spent in the manor as Papa's wife. She had been stitching a leaf pattern onto a handkerchief as part of her dowry and she pricked her finger. Three drops of blood fell on the windowsill. The red of the blood was bright against the white snow and black ebony window and she wished for a daughter with lips as bright as blood, skin as pale as snow, and hair as black as ebony."

I looked at Snow, her dark haunting eyes, her pale, delicate complexion, and the deep, enticing red of her lips. Her silk spun skin was flushed and smudged with dirt, her black hair a wild mess, dampened with sweat. "That's exactly what she got."

Snow laughed. "Elise and Dana probably made it all up so they would have a story to tell a small, fussing child. I think it was the only story they knew. The Southern Ridges are warm. Handmaidens from there aren't used to spending so many winter nights by the fire, looking for things to fill the silence with."

"Otto's bride is from there." Trouble said. "The Southern Ridges."

Snow blinked. "He's marrying the princess of the Southern Ridges? That would make her my mother's niece. My cousin."

Trouble nodded. "Her name is Ava. Otto was betrothed to her mother when they were children."

"The girl with freckles." Snow said. "Otto told me about her. I didn't know she was my mother's sister."

I eyed her curiously. Neither she nor Otto had ever said anything to me about a betrothal before he had been cursed.

Snow grew silent again after that. The forest became unfamiliar as we trekked forward. It was an eerie sensation to be standing beneath trees almost the same as our part of the forest, like being hugged by someone else's grandmother who we'd only just met. I wondered what their music sounded like. If it were more hollow here, less crowded as the trees thinned around us. Perhaps the music here had a more melody and less harmony. There were less squirrels here too. More field mice. I wondered if their energy was less frantic than the mice in our forest.

My thoughts surprised me. It had been so long since I had wondered about the music of the forest. Not since I had stopped being able to hear it.

Not hear it. Be it. Once I and the music of the forest had been one and the same. It felt so long ago.

I grew weary as the afternoon wore on. My feet grew sore and stiff. Snow's steps became slower beside me as she walked with her hand wrapped tight in mine. The sun filtering through the trees faded slowly and dark began to set in.

Trouble was the first to suggest we make camp. We found a clearing large enough for a good fire and two women and a hobgoblin to lie down in. The distant gurgle of a river bubbled in our ears as Snow set to work clearing a place for the fire. Trouble and I scoured the area fallen branches. Leaves crunched beneath my feet as I crouched to reach a fallen oak branch.

A gurgling river. Crunching leaves. The scurrying of field mice in the bushes. The sounds of a forest. I wondered again what music this forest made beneath. An ache set into my chest. A longing for what I had lost. Did I dare look for it? Did I dare listen for the song inside these trees?

I glanced over at Snow. She had finished clearing our camp and was setting to work lighting the kindling.

"Why don't you light the fire?" Trouble asked me.

I blinked, pulling myself out of my thoughts. I turned towards him with a wry smile. "Because I want to make dinner." Let him risk Snow's cooking if he dared.

The hobgoblin shook his head. His beard grazed back and forth across his chest. "That's not what I mean, Red Witch. Why don't you light it the way you used to?"

Had he seen my thoughts a moment ago? Did he know I was longing for the forest's song?

I snatched an oak branch off the ground, scowling at him. "I told you. I'm not a witch anymore."

He stared at me from beneath his thick, bristly eyebrows, stern and unyielding as if he knew the truth. As if he knew that ever since Boris had raped me, since Lucille had tried to rip out my heart, since I had drained every last drop of my powers to summon the help of the forest and sing through Lucille's curse, I had only ever tried to touch my magic once. The connection was broken and I let it stay broken. I had no need for magic. No need for the curses and complexities it brought with it.

"A witch isn't something you can stop being." Trouble said again.

I turned away from him and finished gathering the firewood.

SNOW

It was cold when I woke. Damp and misty. My limbs were sore from sleeping on the ground and the long walk the day before. I pulled myself up. Trouble was asleep a few paces away, snoring like a woodcutter. Birds chirped in the trees around us. It was nice to wake to their music, unmuffled by the cottage walls. Almost as if I were a part of it, mingling in harmony with the peaceful gurgle of the nearby river. The rhythm of Trouble's snores kept time, deep and steady like the beat of a drum. I breathed deep, letting the crisp morning air seep through me as I enjoyed the music.

My stomach grumbled. I got up and searched the camp for our food satchel.

The remains of our night's fire glittered in the morning sun. The wood was charred black like the ebony windows of Papa's manor. Papa had liked them that color. "The color of the void." He would say "The color of possibilities."

What a long time ago that was and yet how close it suddenly seemed. I could almost feel Papa's arms around me as I sat on his lap. Could almost see the red wax drip as he sealed one important letter after another. "Questions, my love." He would say when I asked what was in the letters. "And answers. And many, many more questions."

I smiled at the memory. How safe I had felt. What little need I had had to be curious and yet how freely I had made my interrogations. Of course a king didn't have time to answer all my questions. Not even for his beloved daughter. Eventually Dana and Elise would scoop me out of his lap and whisk me away to my chambers to study music, history, heraldry, and how to hold a fork properly at dinner.

Until I managed to slip away from them with a book of old tales in one hand and an apple in the other and hide myself away in the quiet, empty cracks of the manor house.

Our food satchel lay on the other side of Trouble, not too far from his long, spindly fingers. I dug in it until I found some of the salted rabbit meat --rich and savory-- and went to look for Rose.

I followed the playful babble of the river until the trees cleared and I could see the rush of water flowing out into a valley. Rose stood on the bank, her feet bare, her long skirt and wild tangles of hair rippling quietly in the breeze.

I nibbled my breakfast as I moved toward her. She stood like a statue with her chin lifted proudly. Her arms were held out in front of her as if holding some invisible person in an embrace. She wobbled, first on one foot, then the other, concentrating on . . . something. She moved deliberately completely impervious to my approach.

She hopped forward, then back. She lost her balance and toppled forward onto the riverbank. Her hair flew up. Water splashed as she landed hard on her hands and knees. She pulled back from it, her eyes wide with shock.

I tried to squelch my laughter but it was a hopeless cause. It erupted from my throat like a fireside ballad, bold and daring. I placed a hand over my mouth to hold it back but that only made me shake more deeply.

Rose turned toward me. Droplets drizzled down the side of her chin. She glared. "Don't you dare laugh. This water is freezing."

"Then why were you teetering around at the edge of it like a drunken acrobat?"

I came to get a drink." She said. "Then I decided to practice the court dances you taught me."

I was standing over her now with dribbles of laughter still leaking through my mouth. I held my hand out to help her up. She wrapped her fingers around mine and I pulled her to her feet.

Her face reddened just a little, like the soft petals of her name. "You'll have to teach me the dances again. I'm afraid I've forgotten them."

I kissed her nose to apologize for laughing. "So have I." I assured her. "It's been so long."

Rose sighed. "I guess we'll both look like drunken acrobats at Otto's balls."

"Perhaps not." I swallowed the last bit of rabbit meat and closed my eyes, trying to remember dance lessons with Dana and Elise. The cold morning breeze whispered over my face as I searched for the right memory.

"Keep your head straight." Dana's voice echoed inside my mind. "Do you want to look like a buffoon at your Papa's balls? You must look elegant so that the lords will want you for their wife."

I remembered shuffling awkwardly, staring down at my feet to make sure the steps were right. Of course I hadn't wanted to look like a buffoon. I had wanted Papa to be proud of me, to step away from the sheriffs and lords he was entertaining long enough to twirl me around. To make me feel alive and beautiful and strong and loved as only he could. He had been killed before I was old enough to dance at a ball. Rose was depending on me to show her how to behave at one but I was as lost as she was. All I really knew how to do was hold my fork right and peek from behind my nurses' skirts to watch the courtiers float by.

I quivered at the memories, realizing how much I wanted to teach Rose to dance. Sharing a piece of my childhood with her would be almost like introducing her to Papa.

With my eyes still closed I placed my free hand behind Rose's waist. Her breath lifted gently up and down beneath her ribs. "The most important thing about dancing is trust." I said. "The steps are important but not as important as the connection you share with your partner. A dance is a language. Every move one dancer makes the other counters with a move of their own. When the communication between our bodies stops the dance ends. Close your eyes."

My own eyes were still closed so I couldn't see Rose obey but I could feel it in the way the weight of her hand pressed more firmly against mine, needing me just a little more for support.

The way I needed her.

When Dana had taught me to dance she had taught me that I was to follow and my partner was to lead but Rose and I were connected much more deeply than that. I chose a step and she followed then she chose the next and I followed her. I spun her, then she spun me. Sometimes she chose two steps or three then it came back to me choosing. We listened intently to each other's movements, moving together, creating a unique pattern with our bodies that belonged only to us. We came close then stepped away and then landed again in each other's arms. If I hesitated too long she filled in the space with a quick, elegant decision and I did the same for her.

Once we began to dance I found I remembered more of the steps Dana had taught me than I thought I would but I wasn't using very many of them. Rose and I created our own steps. We moved together, first right, then left, then back, then forward. There was no form to our movements. No frame.

We danced with pure impulse, reading each other's movements and desires just like when we made love in the warmth of our cottage loft.

Were our movements elegant? Were they graceful? I have no idea what they would have looked like to anyone watching but to us they felt perfect. We swayed and twirled and wove, completely engrossed in one another's movements.

Water splashed up from the stream as our feet shuffled against the edge, tickling our chins and neck. We rocked with the flow of the water, rushing past in a thick, steady hum. Rose kept me on my toes, as I wondered where she would swing me next. I remained poised ready to counter her whims with a twist of my own. The wind played music for us as it rustled its way through the trees and hummed a crisp, cold melody in our ears.

"There you great big clodhoppers are."

Rose jolted to a stop. I tried to slow my momentum but I was mid-swing and barreled straight into her chest. We both lost our balanced and toppled over into the river.

The water bit against my skin like ice. It soaked into my skirt and sleeve and hair. I gasped, gripping at Rose for support. I opened my eyes to see the same expression of shock and betrayal on Rose's face.

We both burst into laughter, shaking almost hard enough to keep warm. We untangled ourselves from each other and pulled ourselves to our feet. My stomach tightened as sound roared out of my mouth in thick, bubbling globs. Unable to speak, I reached to ring the water out of my skirt. Droplets streamed onto the riverbank as I squeezed the fabric tight in my hands. My teeth chattered.

"Well." Rose said. "We might both look like drunken acrobats at Otto's wedding but at least we'll be dry inside his ballroom."

Trouble crossed his arms, staring at us as if we'd gone mad. "Will the pair of you stop wasting time and help me pack up camp?"

Rose and I huddled together for warmth and followed him back to the clearing.

The wind rippled over the fields almost like the gush of the river as we followed it toward the mountains. By the end of the first day we could no longer see the woodlands behind us. Only the mountains lifted in a distant, hazy curve on the horizon, as if they had been painted there with a few soft brush strokes. The air was colder without the trees to protect us from the wind. We huddled beneath our cloaks, bracing ourselves against it's bite.

"It's a longer journey if we follow the river." Trouble said "But our backs are breaking as it is with all this firewood to carry. If we had to carry water as well we'd never make it over the mountain before the first snowfall."

Rose shrugged. "You're the seasoned journeyman."

Trouble grunted with pride and we followed his lead.

We ambled across the rolling ripples of grass in silence, trying to keep up with Trouble's hurried pace. "How do you move so fast with such little legs?" Rose asked him the third time she demanded we rest for a sip of water. He glowered at her.

The flatlands stretched for days. No matter how far we walked we never seemed to get closer. As the days wore on our bodies strengthened and it became easier to keep up with Trouble's relentless pace. Rose complained less and we even found the energy to practice our dance steps before going to sleep each night. Trouble laughed at us, insisting we looked like broken puppets despite our synchronicity.

We waited until we'd almost run out of turnips and salted rabbit before I set out my traps.

"No sense carrying more than we have to." Trouble insisted.

Neither of us argued. We were glad to feel our packs lighten each day but it was risky using our last turnip in the hope that we'd be able to lure a rabbit while we slept. The first night all three traps were left empty. Our stomachs rumbled angrily at us all day the next day. I was careful to lay the traps more strategically the next evening, concealing them as deep into the folds of the slopes as possible so that the rabbits would feel protected when they saw the tempting bits of turnip.

Trouble had finished setting up camp when I returned to the others. Rose stood next to the stream, constructing a makeshift fishing pole out of string and a long piece of kindling. I helped her find a water bug to pin to the end of the string but we were too far north to find many fish this late into the autumn. The water bug died on his own from thrashing around to get off the string and night set in around us with no bites.

"I thought you were supposed to be the Huntsman's Apprentice." Trouble grumbled. "Nothing can escape you once you've decided to make the kill."

I glanced at Rose, confused.

"Trouble says Otto's court has made a legend of you." She explained.

"Because Hans taught me to hunt?" I asked, remembering my gruff silent teacher. He had only taught me for a few short weeks but he had been the only person to offer me comfort in those long, lonely days after Papa's death. His lessons had been my salvation. A place to ground myself as I crawled my way out of my grief. He had saved my life more times than I could count. Rose's too. Before Boris killed him.

"Because he taught you to kill." Trouble said.

I flinched at the comment. Hans had killed hundreds in Lucille's service, many of them children. Apart from Boris he had been her favorite errand runner.

"I only kill animals." I said.

Boris and Lucille didn't count. They had behaved like animals.

Trouble pulled his pipe out his mouth. His tobacco stores were not suffering even if our food stores were. He blew a smoke ring out of his mouth and looked at me with a rare serious expression. "Try getting the court to believe that. The Red Witch and the Huntsman's Apprentice. You two are talked about more than the bride herself."

Rose groaned. "Just what we need. Another reason for them to gawk at us." She glared. Hunger was making her testy and I knew she hated being called the Red Witch since she had lost her magic. If she still had it she might have lit him on fire.

Trouble managed to brew us a very thin nettle broth and we went to sleep with our stomachs still rumbling like thunder. I woke in the night from dreams I couldn't remember to find Rose flailing in my arms. I pulled away from her and let the nightmare pass. It seemed worse than usual. She gasped in her sleep and I could see the damp drops of sweat on the soft curves of her face. A single wolf howled in the distance.

That was odd. Wild wolves usually traveled in packs.

At last the dream passed and Rose's sleep became peaceful. I pulled her back into my arms but couldn't manage to fall asleep. Once the green glow of dawn peaked out of the sky I got up and went to check the traps.

The first one was empty. I pulled the grass and weeds away to find the turnip bits untouched,. The little wooden latch still propping up the cage. Disappointment dropped inside my belly. I slipped the turnip bits into my pocket and tied the trap to a string around my belt.

The turnip bits were missing from the second trap but whatever animal had eaten them had managed to escape without triggering the latch.

I approached the last trap with apprehension, hardly daring to hope. Inside was, not one, but three rabbits. A mother and her two almost grown kittens. With a sigh of relief I pulled them out, one at a time, and slit their throats. When they had stopped twitching in my hands I slung them over my shoulder and took them back to camp.

It took half the day to skin and gut the little beasts but the lost time was worth it to have warm, seared rabbit for dinner. Rose and Trouble even managed to catch a fish while they waited for me to finish with the rabbits. We left at dawn the next morning with full bellies and food to last another day.

The next day we ran out of firewood. We huddled together in the dark, trying to protect each other against the cold. Even Trouble, despite his grumbling and half-hearted protests. None of us slept well. We were all up at the first hint of light, glad to have the blood flowing through our veins again to keep us warm.

The mountains seemed to loom ahead of us, never getting nearer until, without warning, we were at their base. The elegant arches lining the horizon disappeared. Instead stony crags and large boulders lined our path as it grew steeper and steeper. The climb was more difficult than the journey on flatland. Even with our journey strengthened legs we had to stop more often to catch our breath.

A light pattering of rain fell from the sky, dampening our cloaks and hair. The wind grew stronger, almost harsh, as it tore through the wet layers of cold. The afternoon wore into dusk as rain continued to drizzle against the earth, softening it beneath our feet. Twice I lost my footing and Rose had to catch me.

Trouble scowled. "We're not making good time. The cave I'd hoped to spend the night in isn't for another two leagues. We won't make it before dark."

I rolled my ankle, smoothing out the muscles where I had tripped.

Rose watched me with concern. "We can look for a ledge against the cliffs." She said. "That will protect us from the wind at least."

I shivered in her arms. Every piece of me was damp. A dry place to sleep was worth a couple hours of walking in the dark. "We can make it to the cave." I said. "If we're careful."

Trouble grunted in agreement. His flesh was thinner than ours, his bones smaller. He wasn't likely to admit it but cold seeped through him much more quickly. I don't know how he was keeping his teeth from chattering.

The rainfall grew heavier as daylight faded. The light grew dimmer and the ground grew slicker. We moved slowly, treading with care. The path was narrow. We walked single file with Trouble in front of me and Rose behind me. The straps on my pack rubbed through the damp fabric of my cloak and shift, biting uncomfortably into my skin. My face and hands were numb from the cold, hardly able to feel themselves. Bushes I couldn't see snatched at my skirts in the dark. I pulled to untangle them.

Something thumped.

Trouble cursed in a language I had never heard before. He stopped. "Devil take that stone! Right in my path. My toe's going to throb for a week now. It would be a good time for you to light a piece of these bushes for a torch, Red Witch, before we all tumble to our deaths."

"Stop calling her that." I came to a halt behind him. "Rose isn't a witch anymore." I turned around for confirmation from Rose.

Rose gasped. Stones rumbled. Her fingers brushed my wrist in the dark and then, in the space of half a breath that felt like eternity, they slipped away.

"Rose!" My own scream spurred me into action. I grasped Trouble tight around the middle and flung myself to the ground. My legs swung over the edge of the mountain, dangling over an abyss of darkness. Mud oozed over my throat and up into my nose and mouth.

I froze in the stillness. Not even my heartbeat. Nothing. I had been too late.

Two hands closed over my ankle, pulling me deeper down into the abyss.

Rose. I began to breathe again. My heart resumed its riotous rhythm.

"Rose." I sputtered through a mouth full of mud as I slid backward on my belly. I gripped Trouble tight, trying to steady myself against Rose's weight, but her pull was stronger than his little hobgoblin body. He skidded backward along with us. I hesitated, considering letting go so that we didn't drag him over the edge with us.

Rose's grip loosened just a little. My heartbeat quickened. "Don't you dare." I shouted. If she was falling I was falling with her. There was no alternative.

The weight of her body slackened.

No. No. No. No. No. I wouldn't let her do it. I opened my mouth to scream again.

"My feet are against the cliff." The sound of her voice was like a bird's song against my ears. Her grip tightened again around my ankle. "If you pull me I can edge my way up."

I tightened my grip on Trouble. He moved forward, dragging me across the ground. Stones scraped against my belly and thighs and chest. My ankle, knee, and thigh ached from the pull of Rose's weight. I gritted my teeth, struggling to hold onto Trouble. Pain burned in my shoulders. I stretched taut between them like a rope pulling a bucked out of a well.

At last my knees touched the ground. I used them to help Trouble move forward, inch by inch, as Rose edged her ways up the cliff. My ankle was numb. I could barely feel Rose's hands wrapped tight around it.

And then my feet were on level ground too. I rolled onto my back and sat up. There were Rose's hands clasped as if in prayer around my ankle. I leaned back, pulling my weight against hers. Trouble threw his little arms around my waist and steadied me. I edged back another inch. There were Rose's wrists. My leg ached at the hip as if it were about to be ripped from my body.

I bent over. The muscles beneath my thighs felt as if they were about to tear open. I closed my palms over Rose's wrists. I held on tight as she released first one hand and then the other from my ankle. She placed her palms down flat on the cliff's edge and began to pull herself up.

A moment later she was in my arms. I leaned onto my back, holding her for a moment, slackening beneath the warm press of her body. I couldn't tell if the tumultuous thumping I heard pounding like the pattering of the rain was my heartbeat or hers. I held her tight, ignoring the pain in my leg.

"Forget the cave." I said. "It's too dangerous to travel in the dark."

A sound almost like a growl escaped Trouble's lips. "It wouldn't be dark if we had a torch."

I couldn't see Rose's expression in the dark but I could tell from the way her muscles tensed just a little that she was glaring at Trouble. "It's too wet for a torch to stay lit." She said.

We moved a few paces from the ledge. I limped on my sore leg and had to lean against Rose for support. There wasn't anything to protect us from the wind or the rain. We plopped down in a wet, slippery patch of grass to wait for morning. I lay with Rose's head rested between my breasts, stroking her hair while Trouble snored beside us.

The rainfall became heavier and heavier. I shivered. Water soaked through my bodice and shift. There was no part of me that wasn't wet. Droplets rippled down my skin, tickling like an insect's crawl. My whole body was numb from the cold. Rose lay next to me with her head rested in the curves of my breasts but not even the soft press of her body could keep me warm. I stroked her hair tenderly, trying to restore some feeling in my fingers as I savored what I had almost lost. She lay still at first then her breathing became short. She began to toss and turn in my arms and I knew she was asleep, out of my reach, gripped by nightmares I could never rescue her from.

An emptiness echoed inside me, aching from the force of my failure. I held her for a moment longer, trying to offer what comfort I could with my touch. She struggled. Her fist came down hard against my cheek and I found that I had feeling in my bones after all. I untangled myself from her, recoiling from the pain.

It wasn't me she meant to hit I reminded myself. It was him inside her nightmares. Boris. The were who had betrayed her friendship and taken her body against her will.

Even though I knew it was true the more I tried to remind myself the harder it was to believe. I had failed to protect her. I had known what a monster Boris was but I had never told her. I had never even mentioned him to her. My silence had harmed so many. Didn't I deserve this pain?

A wolf howled in the distance as if summoned by my thoughts of weres. I shuddered and reached for my knife. The sound was too far off to be any real threat but it still made me jumpy. I gripped the knife in my hand and watched the rain pour down on us from the night sky.

Rose slept fitfully. I didn't sleep at all.

The night stared at me. Still. Empty. Uncertain. The stars were hidden by clouds and rain. Only a tiny hint of moonlight crept through the force of the storm, so faint I couldn't be certain I wasn't imagining it. Wind hissed continuously in my ear until the cold, swirling whisper sounded like silence. Time steeped my mind, infusing it until it seemed to disappear altogether. All there was was night. All there was was cold. I didn't even notice when the rain stopped and the wind began to lessen.

Rose flopped from side to side in the wet grass, moaning. The wolf howled again, closer this time. I closed my grip over my knife hilt. The silver engraving pressed deep into my palms.

Just a wolf, I reminded myself. No were would live this deep into the wilderness so far from any castles or villages. They took wolf form when they chose but at the core they were still human and needed human company as much as any of us.

But why was there only one? Wild wolves traveled in packs.

I watched Rose. Her face was only a shadow in the dim light of the moon. That howl again, long and deep. Strong. Solitary.

The moon was only a sliver through the clouds. Weeks away from being full. It would be difficult, almost impossible for a were to maintain his beast form.

If it was a were, which it wasn't. Not this far out into the wilderness.

Still, it felt as if Rose were pulling her nightmares out of her sleep so that I couldn't even protect her when she woke.

Boris was dead, I reminded myself. I had killed him myself with the same knife I held in my hands. The same knife Hans had given me.

I wish it were that simple. Rose's words echoed in my memory. I shuddered. I only killed animals.

No. That wasn't quite true. Boris had been worse than an animal. As a human he had known he was inflicting pain. He had acted from a cruel selfishness that went far beyond the survival instincts of an animal. I was glad he was dead. Glad I had killed him. I never felt that way with the animals I killed.

Did that make me a killer or a hunter?

The howl sounded again, closer even than before. My heart rattled like old bones inside my breast, deaf to reason. My foot and shoulder ached, throbbing at the memory of Boris's teeth sinking into them. I pulled myself onto my feet, fighting against the memory and scanned the night for movement. The grass patch we were sleeping on was level but completely exposed on all sides without even a bush or large stone to shield us. I spun around, almost dizzy from the speed of the movement.

I gripped my knife. Rational or not I wouldn't wait to strike.

A shadow moved. A low growl like stone against stone. So close I knew I could reach out and touch the creature. I turned to face it.

Was that the outline of his teeth in the dark? His long pointed ears?

But there was no mistaking the eyes that stared at me, almost glowed in the night. A hungry, amber tinted yellow.

"Boris." The word leapt from Rose's lips. I turned toward her as she jolted up, her eyes open.

I turned back to the creature, ready to strike, but he was gone. I spun around in the darkness, trying to find where he had gone but there was no trace of him.

Rose's eyes fell on the knife in my hand. "It was just a dream." She said. Her voice was foggy with sleep.

I shook my head. "I saw a were."

Rose rubbed her eyes. She shook her head. "It was just a dream. No weres would live this deep in the wilderness. We're at least two days from any villages."

"He was howling." I insisted. I hadn't imagined it. I knew I hadn't.

Rose shook her head again. She yawned. "Just a regular wolf then. We'll keep an eye on Trouble in case he comes back." She glanced at the sleeping hobgoblin next to us. He was an inviting size for a wolf's meal. Much easier to kill than two full sized women.

Kill. The word sounded so final. As if a dead man could no longer touch the living and yet . . .

Rose stood up. She stepped toward me and wrapped her arms around me. Our wet clothes pressed between us. I could feel her pulse, almost as fast as mine from the rush of her nightmare, but it began to slow as she placed her chin on my shoulder. I melted into the comfort of her touch.

She was right. She had to be. I had been letting the fear of her nightmares infiltrate my perception. I was letting the dark, solitude of night run wild with frightening memories of things that were gone. Dead. Killed.

And yet . . .

Those hungry, amber eyes stared at me from inside my memory. I shuddered.

ROSE

When morning came we could see the plainlands we had traveled across. The thick blanket of pale green was traced with a small thread of blue stretching outward until it met with a darker, denser green. Our forest. After that the gray and purple colored moorlands stretched on along with the thin thread of the river until they met a bigger patch of blue and silver. The great lake.

How small it all looked. As if we were only a few short steps from home. I glanced again at the darker patches of green with a pang of homesickness for our warm little loft. Our garden. Our beehive. Greta's village. Even the manor. All the places we knew with such intimacy. If anyone had ever asked me if I wanted to explore other parts of the world I would have told them that I did. Yet, standing here on the mountain, cold, hungry, tired, sore from my tumble over the cliff the day before, I felt enveloped in an unwelcoming strangeness. All I wanted was to go home.

"It's beautiful isn't it?" Snow breathed beside me. "This high up it's almost like we could put our tongues out and lick the clouds."

Her tone was filled with such awe that I didn't have the heart to tell her my own thoughts had been more cynical. I turned toward her.

"You have a bruise." I touched her cheek. A deep brown patch I hadn't noticed in the dark lay across the bone. It looked like someone had hit her.

She winced. I pulled my hand away.

Snow held my gaze but her eyes grew distant. Like puddles in the dark. "I must have got it on the cliff ledge when we were pulling you up."

Something in her tone told me that she wasn't telling the truth. My brow wrinkled but I didn't press for more.

I wondered suddenly what the music of a mountains sounded like. Would magic echo more from up here? Would it taste more open? More solid because of the stones? I held still for a moment. Not listening exactly but ready to listen. Wondering what it would feel like if I did.

There was no breakfast to make. No fire to put out. No camp to clean up. As soon as Trouble woke we began our journey again, drudging forward as dawn brightened into morning.

Higher up the mountain we could see more than our forest and the southern moorlands. To the east were more and more mountains, each taller and rockier than the last. To the west, after another patch of forest, far denser and thicker than ours was a glittering blanket of blue almost as pale as the sky. "The Ocean." Trouble called it. "Like a lake but a thousand times bigger and full of salt."

Snow couldn't stop staring at it. "I've read about it." She breathed but I never thought it would be so . . . so big."

Hunger and fatigue did not seem to bother Snow. She marveled at the vastness of the sky, the song of the wind, the dark brown the rain had colored the earth. It was as if the frightened girl clutching her knife who I had stayed up half the night with no longer existed. Instead there was this blissful, wide-eyed mountain nymph in absolute awe of everything she saw. She wasn't even limping even though I knew she had hurt her leg in our fall.

"Who knew the whole world could be so big?" She asked. "Who knew it could be so beautiful?"

"Who knew it could be so cold?" I asked.

Trouble snorted his agreement.

I welcomed the change in Snow but it worried me. Nightmares didn't disappear just because the sun came out. Not completely. My eyes kept straying to the bruise across her cheek as we walked. I was almost certain I had hit her in my sleep. I shuddered at the thought. She might have forgiven me for it but it was hard to forgive myself. How could I comfort her in the dark if it were my ghosts that were harming her?

My nightmares had been getting worse out here in the wilderness. I was starting to remember pieces of them. Lucille's poison holding me still. Boris's yellow wolf eyes. I resented the memories. Let them haunt my sleep if they must but my waking hours were my own. I didn't want my past leaking into them.

I was the first to spot the castle. The aisles of stones around us cleared long enough for us to see the top of the mountain. Cleanly cut stone protruded out of the mountain top as if it were a part of the same structure. The walls were precise, almost delicate compared to the crags that surrounded them. Torrents rose in uniform patterns along each side. It was strange to see something so carefully crafted nestled inside the wild unpredictability of the terrain. I wondered if it were as silent and cold inside as the manor had been the one night I had stayed in it. The manor could have been a village house in comparison to this cluster of buildings. It was more like a city but far more elegant and imposing with two rings of fortified walls cluttered with guard towers.

I stood staring at it, transfixed to the spot for reasons I could not have explained if I had tried. Snow stopped beside me. I pulled my eyes away from the majestic structure and turned toward her, expecting her wide eyes to be filled with as much awe as I felt.

She gave me a little half smile. "Trouble said we'll be there tomorrow. Warm food and a warm bed. I can't wait."

"And a bath." I added. Snow and I were both coated in so much dirt that our skin was two shades darker. We hadn't been able to wash since we had stopped following the stream at the foot of the mountain. All the water from the rain had only soaked the dirt deeper into our skin.

She kissed my cheek. "The faster we move the sooner we will get there." She turned and scurried after Trouble who hadn't even stopped to glance at the castle. I could see his little legs moving forward in quick, gaping strides as his pace nearly doubled.

I knew she was right but I stayed where I was for another moment, staring at the castle. A strange, quiet feeling I couldn't quite describe had come over me, ominous and familiar. Somehow I couldn't imagine this castle being as silent and cold as the manor. I imagined it to be busy and musical, bubbling with laughter. So different than Snow and I's cottage in the wood and yet so uncannily . . . familiar.

My heart fluttered. We're almost there. Almost home.

Home? The thought surprised me. We couldn't be further from home. I must have been hungrier and colder even than I'd realized. A warm feeling stirred inside me as if I were tasting the memory of a dream.

"Rose? Are you coming?" Snow's voice was a long way off. I could no longer see her and Trouble through the twists and turns of the foliage in front of me. I turned and stumbled after them.

A thin woodland scattered over the mountain terrain and soon obscured our view of the castle. The trees were spread apart, most of them still young. I wondered what their song sounded like. Wind chimes maybe, light and spritely. Could I try to listen, just to see if my soul could still open to the wild? I paused for a moment. Quiet. Ready.

I shook the thought out of my mind. There was no point in pining after my magic. It was gone. I didn't want it back.

The wind picked up as we walked, creating it's own song. Almost a howl as it swirled through the trees and our hair and skirts. Perhaps that was the sound Snow had mistaken for wolves. Trouble led us downward for a ways then upward again. I looked around, feeling strangely oriented for a moment before I realized we had stumbled upon a path. Dusk fell through the shadow of the trees. The last traces of light trickled down in a woven texture of gold. My tumble over the cliff had taught us not to travel after dark. We stopped to make a fire.

We had already eaten the last of the rabbit and pike but at least the rain had stopped. Enough of the surrounding woodland had dried for us to gather kindling. Snow used her knife to gnaw off a few of the more stubborn branches to make a good, healthy fire. Trouble used the last of our water from the water skins to make a warm nettle broth. It helped heat our insides but did nothing to quiet the rumbling in our stomachs. Hungry, but as warm as we could expect to be, we huddled up and went to sleep.

The sight of the castle was the last thing than ran through my mind before I collapsed inside my head, dreaming.

I lay in a bed. The sheets were made of silk. Soft. Warm. Someone was humming. I couldn't see them. The bed was surrounded by sheer, silk curtains. Rose petals sprinkled down from above, falling around me in a slow, sticky rain.

The humming stopped.

"Like her name."

That was Gran's voice. Sweet like honey. Strong like oak.

A hand pulled back the curtains. A giant hand the size of my face. It was covered in ink stains.

"Let's show her the bear. She will like the dancing."

Another voice. Familiar. Warm. Deep.

Laughter. Light and giddy like crystal. This third voice was so charming that it didn't even have to say anything to turn everyone's attention towards its owner. And I didn't have to see everyone to know that everyone's gaze had left the bed and fallen on her.

"Rest my love." The deep familiar voice said. "Don't over tax yourself."

I stood up in the bed. It expanded around me, making room for my full height.

A bear tapped me on the shoulder. I turned around. It was the red bear Otto had been before he'd been Otto. He wore the blue waistcoat Snow had made for him. He bowed and held out his paw. "Let's dance." He said.

"I don't know how." I said

But that didn't seem to matter. The next moment we were dancing. We floated across the silk sheets as they expanded around us, stretching out into the horizon until all I could see was silk. Only it wasn't silk anymore. It was an endless forest of clouds as my bear-brother and I floated through the sky.

We spun and wove, drifting higher and higher until, finally, we stopped.

"Look down." Otto said.

Below us, the clouds parted just wide enough that we could see the castle. I could see the layers of walls stretching all the way around the keep, the stables, the kitchens, the gardens, even an orchard. There were six guard towers and three layers of walls. Inside the innermost ward, next to the keep, was not a chapel but a cathedral. It stretched up into the sky with elegantly pointed towers, ornately painted glass windows, and intricately carved statues of animals entwined with long thorny vines. A bell sounded from one of the towers.

"Welcome home." Otto said.

I opened my eyes. It was dawn. Trouble snored from the other side of the remains of the fire. Snow was twisting and turning fitfully beside me.

I sat up. Had I really just dreamt a dream that wasn't a nightmare? It had been months since I'd been able to do that. At least not one I remembered.

I stared at the sky, letting the dream linger for a moment, then I stood up and did what I could to smooth the tangles out of my curls with my fingers. My belly rumbled persistently, making it hard to concentrate. At last I gave up. Forget my stupid hair. I was going to find something to eat.

I wasn't a hunter like Snow but if I were lucky there might be some truffles or blackberries nearby. I thought about trying to invoke my magic - to tune myself to the woods and feel through it for something edible -but my whole body shuddered at the idea. All my nightmares threatened to return in one instant.

I pulled away from the temptation. Even as hungry as I was I couldn't ransack through the forest's spirit in order to use it for my own gain. Not again. Not the way I had done when I had killed First-Light's mother.

I scanned the bushes, looking for any signs of blackberry leaves. I ran my eyes across the ground, searching for truffles. The only thing I saw were pinecones and nettles and ferns. Beautiful, but useless to my belly.

I couldn't stray too far from Trouble and Snow. I didn't want them to panic when they woke. At last I gave up with a big, exasperated sigh and turned around.

I scrutinized the trees a second time as I passed them. Except for a few pines scattered here and there their leaves had almost all lost their green. Most of them were ash trees, thin and brittle with only a few brown, crisp leaves still clinging to their branches. I stopped in front of an odd looking tree with smooth, gray-brown bark. Its few remaining leaves were a deep brilliant gold.

I groaned. The pointed shape of the leaves meant it was a fruit tree. If Otto had decided to get married in the spring instead of early winter we could have feasted this morning.

I heard a coo then a rustle. I looked up. A partridge flew out of the tree. My eyes drifted to where it had been perched. A nest.

I hesitated. It was unlikely that the partridge would lay eggs this late in the year but not impossible. What did I have to lose by checking? I pulled off my boots, shivering as the chill of the morning nipped at my toes. I reached for the lowest branch then used it to pull myself up into the tree. I wasn't as nimble at climbing as Snow but I managed. A moment later I was balanced on one of the wider branches, staring down into the nest.

There were eggs. Twelve of them, little and speckled.

My insides did a dance. I tried not to think about the likelihood that they were fertilized, and scooped them into my apron pockets. It would be almost impossible to climb down without breaking them but if I jumped down and landed on my feet perhaps it would not jostle them too much. I swung my legs over the branch, preparing myself for the drop.

I froze.

Leering up at me from beneath the tree with a big toothy grin was the hungry face of a forester.

"Hello girly." His grin widened. I had the eerie sensation that I had seen him before. "That's quite a rump you've got. Need help getting down?"

My heartbeat quickened. All my nightmares crowded around me once again. Memories of Boris. Of Lucille's poison. Of . . .

I opened my mouth but no sound came out. All I saw was Boris. It was as if I was there instead of here, held still once again by Lucille's poison, unable to defend myself, to run, to say no.

"Don't fret girlie." The man winked. "It's not your eggs I'm after." He laughed a big, booming laugh at his own joke.

I felt nauseous. I felt Boris's hands on me as he pulled me up to his chamber.

"Come on now." The man said when I didn't move. His tone was more commanding now. He held out his hand. "Come on down. Make a man happy and I'll see that you're fed good and proper."

I stayed where I was, finding it more and more difficult to keep my balance on the branch. I had seen him before. I know I had. Why was my mind so clouded? I couldn't think properly. I opened my mouth again to tell him to go to hell but my voice wasn't working. What was wrong with me? I wasn't drugged this time. I shouldn't be so afraid.

He waggled his eyebrows. "Even a scruffy ragamuffin like you is good for a tumble. You'll earn your dinner right enough. A bed too if you can show me you're worth having again tomorrow."

Then I remembered where I'd seen him before. His voice carried through my memory. *Pity. She's old enough for a tumble.* I hadn't seen anything but his boots at the time, lying, as I had been, in the straw of Lucille's tower, pretending to be dead. He'd come to fetch my heart from Greta and had plagued her with his lewd suggestions.

"Alf."

Trouble's voice. I turned my head to see the hobgoblin emerge along the path, followed by Snow.

"Run back to the castle. Tell the king that The Red Witch and The Huntsman's Apprentice have arrived. They would like a carriage and a hot meal."

Alf stepped back. He looked at the hobgoblin then at Snow, then at me. His face was white like bones. He opened his mouth then closed it. At last he bowed his head. "Right away, your lordship." He said and scurred away.

I stared after him until he was completely out of sight. My fists clenched. My jaw held tight. It wasn't until he was gone that I realized I'd been holding my breath. I hated that I was still shaking. I had been safe up here in the tree. He couldn't reach me. Why had I been so afraid?

Snow looked up at me curiously from the ground. "Are you alright Rose?" She turned to look in the direction Alf had gone with murder in her eyes. "I don't like the way he was looking at you."

Good. She hadn't heard anything he'd said. I didn't want Snow running after him with her knife.

"I found some partridge eggs." I found my voice at last. "Let me hand them down to you so they don't break."

We were all hungry enough to eat nettles. We barely had the patience to let Trouble make a fire so we could boil the tiny little partridge eggs. When they were finished we gulped them down, still hot enough to burn our tongues, almost without chewing. They were small but still nourishing and we all felt better once they were in our bellies. We had hardly begun to put out the fire and pack up the pots when we heard the rattling of the royal carriage making its way toward us.

It was an impressive sight. An elaborate structure of carved oak, dancing with depictions of birds and vines and pulled by two white mares with gold harnesses. Their hooves stomped against the earth beaten path as the carriage rattled its way toward us. It came to a stop.

Otto leaped out of the carriage grinning. I barely had time to stand up before his arms were wrapped around me in a warm, tight circle. He pulled away and didn't seem to care that the dried mud still covering my dress was now smudged across his white silk shirt and gold coat.

Snow came up beside me and flung her arms around his neck. Otto laughed. There was a tint of pink across his cheeks as he stepped back. He cast me a sheepish glance then his warm smile returned. The sunlight glinted across the gold circlet on his head. Combined with his mess of red curls it looked almost like fire. He beamed at us, then looked down at Trouble. "Alf said you lot were hungry."

Trouble took the last swig of water from the water skin and wiped his beard with the back of his hand. The dirt caked to his face smudged across his nose and onto his cheek. "Hungry. Frozen. Parched to the bone. But I've brought the two milksops, as you can see." His shoulders rose just a little with the pride of a job well done but his habitual glower never left his face.

Otto gestured toward the carriage. "Come. I've brought you a feast fit for -well" The sheepish look returned to his face and he grinned. "A king."

Otto opened the carriage door and guided us inside. I sank onto the soft velvet seats. I'd never sat on anything so soft before. It was warm inside too. The walls protected us from the wind as we huddled together in the small space.

Otto passed us a strudel, still warm from the kitchen and drizzling with a sweet cherry glaze. Then he gave us roasted swan along with a flagon of wine to quench our thirst. I'd never had wine before. The liquid dribbled down my throat, rich and heavy. My insides lit up with warmth and I felt as if I wanted to dance and sleep at the same time. I grinned at Otto. Maybe having a king for a brother wasn't all bad.

The carriage lurched and few minutes later we were jostling up the road as the wheels creaked and turned beneath us. It was an odd sensation. To be traveling and resting at the same time. I gazed out the window, watching the trees drift past. A moment later I was asleep.

It was dusk when I woke. The carriage had stopped. I pulled back the velvet curtains to peer out at the buildings that surrounded us. A keep towered above us, at least six stories high. A horse whinnied from inside a long building that must have been the stables. Narrow alleyways stretched out in every direction. There weren't many people moving about this late. Only the guards. They still wore the same plain black tunics that they had worn when they had been in Lucille's service. I glanced at Snow quickly enough to see her shudder.

"It's so much bigger than Papa's Manor." She said. "I think I will get lost."

Otto winked. "I won't let you get lost. You'll love the library. It's in the cathedral."

"Cathedral?" I asked, remembering my dream. How had I known there was a cathedral? Trouble must have mentioned it during the journey. I glanced around for the hobgoblin but he was nowhere to be seen. He had already scampered off to find his brothers.

Otto helped us out of the carriage and led us into the keep. It was dark inside. He lifted a candelabra from the wall and led us through the main hall towards the staircase. A faint brush of music and laughter trickled over our ears. My pace lingered as the hypnotic lull of the music scraped softly against my ears. Light streamed out of a doorway, illuminating a cluster of paintings.

I stopped. The sly smile of a woman in red velvet stared at me from one of the paintings. The familiarity of the woman's red curls and delicate nose perplexed me.

Snow gasped. "She looks just like you."

Otto smiled. "That's mother. Queen Dehlia. 'The vixen', jealous nobles called her. She was a scullery maid before father fell in love with her and made her his queen."

The likeness was uncanny. It was strange to see myself dressed up like a queen, reclining on a chaise lounge as if she belonged there. "I'm taller." I pointed out, though it was hard to tell for sure with her seated. "She was a scullery maid?"

"It created quite a scandal." Otto said. "She dressed in gold slippers and pretended to be nobility. By the time father found out he was already so in love with her he didn't care who she was and married her anyways. The court hated her for it at first but then they too fell under the spell of her charm."

I stared at her. A strange, distant warmth stirred inside me. "Did they make a statue of her?" I asked. "A fox covered in rose vines?"

"Yes." Otto sounded perplexed. "How did you know?"

But I couldn't answer him. How *had* I known?

Unless . . .

Could I have remembered?

SNOW

Otto took his leave of us to join the rest of his guests as they gathered in the hall for their nightly festivities. Rose and I were led to a series of rooms clustered together on the fourth floor. Past the anteroom there was a bedroom and a closet and a balcony. Each room was the size of our cottage, covered in tapestries and paintings and curtains. My eyes swam, trying to make sense of the rich colors and ornate designs. The size of the rooms made me feel small and exposed. Had it really been so long since I had been in Papa's manor house that the opulence of a castle frightened me?

But none of the chambers in Papa's manor had been quite this big.

A fire blazed in the fireplace, creating a piece of warmth despite the cold, stone walls. Two chests were pressed against the wall inside the closet. I wondered if Otto thought we had actually brought -or owned- that many belongings or if they were already full of fine clothing for his balls and feasts. I placed our small sack -mostly empty since we had eaten all the food -on top of one of the chests. My traps jangled against the wood through the fabric. I peeked inside to make sure our extra sets of clothes were still separating the traps from the soft surface of my mother's silver. It would be strange to have occasion to wear them. I had been too young for such fine jewelry when Lucille had taken them from me.

The servant who had led us here left, leaving us in the care of a stern, elderly woman who introduced herself as Louisa. She drew us a bath inside

40

the closet with water boiled over the fire. Rose and I both moved to help but she waved us away with a quick, piercing gaze. We watched as she poured the water into the basin. Steam lifted from the ripples.

At last Louisa had finished pouring the last bucket into the bath. She set it down next to the fire and looked up at me. "Is there anything else I can do for you, your majesty?"

I blinked. Your majesty. It had been so long since anyone had called me that. Not since long before I had given up Papa's kingdom to Otto. It felt like a ghost's moan against my ears. A bitter piece of my past reaching for me with cold, icy hands. I froze, unable to speak.

"Your majesty?" Louisa pressed, still waiting for me to answer.

I stared at her. She stared back, puzzled, concerned.

"That will be all for tonight." Rose said.

Louisa bowed and took her leave. I watched as she swept out into the bedroom and closed the door behind her. I stared at the deep stained oak door half expecting it to -

What? Open with a plate of poisoned sausages? Lead me down into Papa's dungeons to watch Lucille torture her prisoners? My heart thundered inside my chest as memory piled on top of memory.

"Snow." Rose's voice, calm and musical. Her touch, soft and warm against my wrist.

I turned toward her. Her gaze fixed on mine, hypnotic as always. We could still hear the soft gurgle of music rising from the hall. Rose smiled. The glint in her golden eyes was wistful. Excited. "Let's bathe for the feast. We'll be late enough as it is."

The memories scattered from my mind, swept away by the wind of Rose's voice, but my heart continued to beat like a battering ram in my chest. I realized suddenly that this was the first time we had been alone together in weeks. The warmth of Rose's hand on my wrist weighed like a feather. It scorched like a flame. I returned her smile. Slyly. Playfully. "I don't want to go to the feast." I said. "There is so much to be done here."

Her smile deepened. The glint in her eyes shown to match mine. She stepped toward me, pulling me toward her in the same motion, and kissed me softly on the lips. Lightly. Teasingly. Like a feather. Like fire. Like a storm. Like the gentle touch of a rose petal.

I reached up and found the lacings of her bodice. Slowly, I began to pull them apart, loosening them first, then pulling the chords out one at a time. My hands lingered on the soft plush of her breasts as I worked. Her kiss deepened, growing hungrier. She reached for my dress, pulling at the strings with a firm, steady motion. A few moments later both of our dresses lay in pools of fabric around our ankles.

I shivered, breaking away from her kiss so that I could take in the the naked curves of her body with my eyes. Her round breasts. Her long legs.

Why did they seem so much more striking when they were uncovered? So much bolder because they were vulnerable. Desire burned through the chills of my own naked body. I didn't feel vulnerable. Not with Rose. I felt free. I felt strong.

Rose laughed. She lifted up a booted foot. It looked big and bulky at the bottom of her slender, naked legs. "These can't go in the bath." She said.

I knelt and unlaced them then pulled them off of her feet. She knelt beside me and helped me with my own boots, unlacing them carefully as if the course wool strings were made of silk.

We both shivered. Our skin bubbled with goosebumps as we climbed into the bath. Warm water spread over us, rippling with the motion of our bodies. We settled into the basin. I let the heat seep through me, reaching down toward my bones. The dirt and stiffness from our journey began to melt away. The pain in my hip from our fall over the cliff lessened. Rose handed me a rag. I took the thick clump of fabric in my hand and dipped it into the water. Droplets ran down my wrist as I pulled it out.

I washed Rose's back first, rubbing gently as the dirt caked onto her skin cleared away. I washed her neck next, then her breasts, her thighs. I caressed carefully, savoring the sensation of our touch beneath the water.

She took the cloth and began to clean me. Her touch was gentle. I felt powerless beneath it like a piece of glass about to shatter. Only I didn't care if I shattered because I was with Rose. If I shattered her presence would pull every fragment back into its place. The water swirled around us, thick like honey. Music wafted from the halls below, reaching a crescendo in its cadence.

"It's like a dream here." Rose murmured as she ran her hands over my shoulder. "It's so vast. So opulent." Her long red curls spiraled down her breasts, not quite managing to cover her nipples. Her skin was pale and luminous, flickering with the light of the fire.

"You are a dream." I said, unable to hold back anymore. I slid toward her, guiding her thighs open as I pulled my own legs apart and tangled them around her. Our thick, grizzly hairs tangled together beneath the water. The rag dropped to the ground with a squishing sound that was barely audible over the rising pant of our breath. She slid her arms around my back, moving them slowly downward. I kissed her softly, then pulled back, checking to make sure it was me she saw, that she wanted this.

Rose moved toward me in the same motion. She thrust her tongue into my mouth, licking greedily, and pushed her whole body against mine. I lost myself in the sweetness of her touch, her scent, her breath. I moved my kisses down from her mouth to her neck, to her breasts, then plunged my head beneath the warmth of the water, letting my hair float up around my ears. The water muffled the sound of Rose's voice as she began to moan from the touch of my tongue inside her. Her voice grew louder, filling the room like a song, until her body tensed, then slackened against the side of the tub. I pulled my head of out of the water, gasping for breath.

No sooner had I come up than her mouth was on mine again, drinking away the sweetness of her own juices. Her fingers traced themselves over my thighs, massaging as they went, and then she had found me, thrusting her fingers in, firm and strong. She pushed harder and harder, satisfying deep inside as I swelled against her touch.

The world stopped. It lit on fire. It sang as only Rose could make it sing. I surrendered to the spasmodic movement of my body, ready to release a scream at any moment and then, at last, my body slackened. I curled into Roses arms, stirring the water slowly, and lay my head groggily against her breasts.

I woke in the bed. Rose must have carried me in after I fell asleep. I wanted to roll over and caress her but she was sleeping peacefully for once. I couldn't risk waking her from the rest she so deeply needed. Instead I gazed at the long slope of her nose, the vibrant pink of her lips, the length of her lashes beneath her lids. As if any amount of her physical beauty could hope to represent the fire inside. Careful not to disturb her, I pulled the layers of blankets back and slid off the bed.

The soft touch of the rug beneath my feet felt odd. Familiar in a way I didn't like. Such luxuries were beyond our means in our cottage. The last time I'd stepped on a rug had been at Papa's manor, when Lucille had locked me in my chamber to starve.

I crept across the bedroom floor with the stealth of a hunter. I opened the door, wincing at the sound of the handle creaking. It led me into the closet. The bathwater hadn't been removed yet but the fire had been put out. I closed the door behind me then rummaged in the chest until I found a shift and gown with lacings simple enough to tie myself. Otto had filled the chests to the brim with clothing fit for his wedding feasts. I fumbled to pull the gown over my head and set to work lacing up the sides. The gown was velvet. I couldn't see the color properly in the dim light but I could feel the rich, soft texture. The sleeves hung loose at my shoulders and tight at my wrists.

At last the lacings were tied. I slid on a pair of slippers that were only a little loose. I wiggled my toes, wishing for the familiarity of my own boots but I didn't know where Rose had put them after she'd pulled them off my feet. Besides, they would cause raised eyebrows if I wore them with a noble's gown.

There was another door on the other side of the closet. It led me into the anteroom where Louisa was sleeping quietly on a chaise lounge.

There was yet another door across the room. I crept carefully over the rug and turned the handle. Slowly. Carefully. All this stealth reminded me of creeping out of my chamber with Constanze guarding me.

Poor, stern faced Constanze who had been executed for feeding me porridge.

I shuddered. Another memory. Another piece of my past creeping into my mind like a worm.

The rooms here were so much bigger than the ones in Papa's manor. Our chambers alone could have been three or four houses from Rose's village. It made me feel small. Like a mouse in a fox's den.

Once out in the hall I could move more freely. I wasn't a captive in this castle, I reminded myself. I was Otto's guest. I was free to roam where I chose.

The corridors were long, lined with paintings of dead kings and queens. More corridors branched in either direction every few feet. I counted my steps, doing my best to remember which way we had been led the night before. At last I came to the staircase leading down into the hall. I descended quickly, winding four stories down, until I reached the castle hall. Light poured in through tall, towering windows. My feet echoed against the stone as I made my way across the hall..

If our chambers had made me feel like a mouse the hall made me feel like a water midge lost in a lake. The ceiling rose up to the top floor of the castle. A balcony from each floor loomed down at me, casting shadows against the marble floor in the faint gray light of the morning. I trudged across the ripples of light until I reached the oak doors on the other side. They too towered over me like the great trees they were made from. A bleary eyed guard unbolted them for me and I stepped out into the ward.

I tried not to shudder at the sight of the guard's plain black tunic. The same tunic the guards had worn under Lucille's service. Had this man come with her to Papa's manor or had he stayed here in her castle? He had curly brown hair and deep blue eyes. They didn't look like the eyes of a killer.

The guard stiffened and I realized I was staring. I nodded my thanks and stumbled out into the ward.

Servants scurried past me with buckets of water, buckets of coal, bundles of chopped wood. I could smell the warm yeasty scent of fresh bread coming from the kitchen mingled with the stink of chamber pots being carried away. A thin blond girl struggled to herd a flock of unruly geese across the cobblestones.

The cold bite of the late autumn morning bit into my bones as I looked around for someone who didn't look too busy. A young boy was leaning against a wall, watching the girl herding geese with an amused expression.

"Which way is the kitchen?" I asked him.

He turned toward me lazily, taking in the gown and slippers. "What do you want with the kitchen?" He asked. "Did a poor maid bring you the wrong kind of cheese?"

I opened my mouth, startled. It was true that some nobles were cruel and hard to please but I'd never met any common folk brave enough to speak to them with such candor.

"Conrad." A voice snapped. I turned to see the thin blond girl facing him with her hands on her hips. Her loose, wool dress draped over her thin features as she glared at the boy with small, dark eyes. Her hair was plaited carefully and wound around her head like a crown. "Show the king's guests some respect and help me with these geese." She turned to me with a curtsy. "The kitchen is that way, My Lady, just east of the keep.".

"Thank you." I nodded and headed in the directed she had indicated. I didn't tell her that it was 'Your Majesty' not 'Your Lady" or ask her why she had curtsied instead of bowed. Her tone had been almost as curt with me as it had been with the boy Conrad despite her chidings for him to be more respectful.

I decided I liked them both. Anything was better than the reserved respect Louisa and the guard had addressed me with. Almost as if I wasn't there at all. I tried not to take notice of how the other servants parted as I made my way through the ward, always making sure they didn't end up in my path. They averted their eyes, trying not to look too close. I knew they meant it as a sign of respect but it made me feel foreign. Isolated. As if I were being rejected from their busy, ordinary lives.

The kitchen was not far. The rich scent of yeast and cinnamon grew stronger and soon I could see the smoke from the ovens rising in the cold morning air.. I quickened my pace. A page scurried past me with his head ducked down. I caught sight of Trouble's youngest brother, Lad, as he burst out of the kitchen with a tray full of strudels. I grinned when I saw him.

"Snow!" He stopped and looked nervously over his shoulder, clutching his tray of strudels. He balanced it on one hand and uncurled and curled one of his long fingers, indicating that I should stoop low to hear him. I did, "Can't stop now." He said. "Sludge'll have my ears. I swear he takes his cooking more seriously than the real reason we're here in the king's service. He's always been fussy about his cooking but it's worse now that he's cooking for lords and ladies. He's crankiest during breakfast too." Lad nodded toward the tray and winked. "Take a Strudel. There's an apple one there in the middle. Lord Bastian won't miss it."

I obediently took the pastry. No sooner had I lifted it off the tray than Lad had scurried off in the direction of the keep. I sighed and sank my teeth into the pastry. The scalding hot filling burnt my tongue. I pushed it away inside my mouth to let it cool.

The cathedral bell sounded, echoing through the whole castle like a warning. Dawn. The last echo of the loud metallic sound faded into the morning. My ears caught another sound. A gruff, low moaning, almost like a growl.

Animal moans were to be expected this close to the slaughter house but this was not a cow or a hen or a sow. It was the deep and gruff and gravely. The familiar moaning of a bear.

I stepped around the corner of the kitchen. Three large domed ovens were lined next to each other. The hobgoblin Sludge stood with a ladle, dripping porridge onto the ground as he shouted orders and tried to argue with two men next to one of the ovens. The top of his head barely reached the center of their shins but his voice echoed with authority.

"No. You can't use one of my ovens to heat coals. I don't care how many cubs you have to train -add the saffron, Ellie, now, before the onions brown -I've got three dozen nobles to feed, not to mention their waiting staff and the usual castle servants -the cherries are done. Get them up to the king before they get cold. You know how he likes his berries -I don't have time to be lending my ovens to anybody."

"Come now, Cook. It's a gift for the king." A scruffy looking man with long black hair and one big gold earring in his left ear said. He held a long stick with a hook attached to it. Next to him stood the forester Rose and I had run into when we'd first arrived. I tensed at the sight of him. Something about him was uncannily familiar.

Behind the men was a wheeled cage with two brown bears locked inside, one grown and the other just a cub. They were thin and grimy. I could smell the scent of their feces locked inside the cage with them. Both bears had gold rings like the one in the man's ear pierced through their noses. The cub pawed at his ring, crying out as he tried to pull it free. It had been newly inserted. I could see bits of blood in the fur near his nostrils. His claws had been taken out. In their place were dark dried, clumps of infecting scabs. His back paws were coated in fresh, pink and white burns. The gnarled flesh oozed with red and white puss.

Dancing bears. My stomach churned, remembering Lucille's iron shoes she'd used to make her prisoners dance. The bear trainers used coals.

The older bear lay inside the cage with his paws over his ears, unmoving. His scabs and burns had healed long ago but I could still see a deep sense of fear and defeat in his eyes as he watched the man with the earing's hooked stick.

There was a shout from inside the kitchen. A girl came running out, pale and pleading. She murmured something to Sludge.

Sludge's eyes flared. "What?" He demanded. "Again? We'll have no flour left at this rate. If I get my hands on that thief I swear I'll cut him to pieces." He darted toward the kitchen door. "Get these men away from my kitchen Ellie." He called over his shoulder." Before they get animal hairs in my strudels."

The bear cub moaned from inside his cage. The girl stood where she was, nervously looking at the two men with her hands behind her back. The forester looked her up and down with hungry eyes. "Ellie, isn't it?" He grinned a big toothy grin. "A right ripe little thing to keep in the kitchen."

And then I recognized him. Alf. Yes. Yesterday in the forest had not been the first time I had seen him. I had seen him before, heating Lucille's iron shoes for her while I watched, hidden in the corner of Papa's dungeon.

I could feel my eyes flashing. My hand reached for where my knife would be if I hadn't been wearing a silly velvet gown. "You heard the cook, gentleman. There is nothing for you here."

The men turned toward me, startled by my presence. The forester bowed his head. I could not see if there was any recognition in his eyes. Surely he knew that I would recognize him as one of Lucille's servants. Had he forgotten that I had lived with her as a child or did he think I wouldn't remember him?

"As her majesty wishes." Alf held a finger to his lips. He winked. "Let's not spoil the king's surprise. "He glanced at the bears in their cage. The cub stopped pulling at his ring. He stuck his head through the bars, looking at me with big round eyes. He turned his head only to realize it was stuck between the two iron poles.

The man with the earring laughed. He placed his hand on the cage and wheeled it away from the kitchen. Alf followed. I watched them go. The cub's little forlorn howls echoed inside my ears. The memory of his burnt and bleeding paws remained like a scar even after the rattle of the cage wheels had faded and all I heard was the noisy clattering and chattering of the kitchen. Ellie pulled some cherry strudels out of the oven beside me.

I looked at the strudel still in my hand. The burn on my tongue stung like a bite of nettles but there was a bite in my stomach that burned more strongly. I wasn't hungry anymore. I set the pastry down next to an oven and turned back toward the keep.

I shivered as I walked. Dawn had risen into full morning and I could see my breath cling to the air like smoke. I stopped. Another sound wafted over my ears.

Deep, haunting notes filled the ward. Voices. Dozens of them, all sounding together, each different, wrapping around each other in a beautifully woven dance. I turned my gaze toward the sound and found myself staring at the tall, majestic towers of the cathedral. The building was overwhelmingly ornate. Tall and stately with elaborate vines and animals carved into the stone. The music echoed around me, seeping into a deep piece of me. A piece I hadn't known was aching. I turned away from the keep, making my way toward the voices instead.

I passed through a menagerie of animal statues made of white stone but I hardly glanced at them. I'd never heard so many voices singing at once. Sweet. Soft. Yet cold somehow. Distant despite the seamless way they blended together. Some deep. Some high like the twittering of birds. As I drew nearer I could hear words in their song but it was in a language I had never learned. The unfamiliarity of the language only made the music more ethereal. Unreal, like something from another world.

I was so entranced by the complexity of the music that I barely noticed the high reaching arches of the cathedral door as I stepped through them. I hardly noticed the sun glittering in through the colored windows like a bright garden of jewels. I hardly noticed the hush of the courtiers and servants lined together on long wooden benches. I hardly noticed the ceiling, almost high enough to be the sky, carved with more intricate images of animals and vines. The singers stood together at the back of the room in long, identical brown robes. Probably the simplest, most humble sight in the room and yet my eyes were transfixed on them as I listened to the sweet, ethereal tapestry of their voices.

Why was I crying?

As quickly as it had begun the music stopped. I emerged from my daze and took full stock of where I was standing at the front of a long isle. A man in a long white robe stepped up in front of the singers. He read the bans for Otto's upcoming marriage then began to talk about the complexities of life. The crowd began to fidget in their seats. Some turned to stare at me. Their gaze made me feel small and out of place. The man in the white robe narrowed his eyes, presumably displeased by the distraction.

I brushed the tears out of my eyes and turned toward the large oak doors I had entered through. They were closed. I was trapped until the sermon was over. I scanned the crowded rows of seats in a panic, looking for somewhere to sit.

A flash of gold silk stirred from the corner of the room. A noble girl rising quietly from her seat. I moved slowly toward the empty seat as she walked away. I stopped just as I reached it, turning to see if she planned on coming back.

The girl stood leaning against the wall, watching the bishop. His voice filled the room, steady and monotonous. I looked at the seat again, then back toward the girl.

She was gone.

I blinked, scanning my eyes up and down the wall, looking for where she might have gone. She was nowhere in sight. There was no trace of gold silk anywhere in the crowd. I looked behind me. The huge oak doors were still closed. Had I imagined her? But there was the empty seat in front of me that hadn't been there before.

Then I saw it. A long straight crack in the wall, running up and down just tall enough for a person to slip through.

A secret door.

My feet moved without asking for my permission. A moment later I stood next to the crack. I looked to make sure no one was watching then pushed the door in. It slid open without a sound and I stepped into a pitch black chamber, leaving only the crack open behind me. I waited, letting my eyes adjust to the darkness. At last I could make out a flight of stairs leading upward and the faintest glow of light in the distance. Was that a flicker of gold fabric swishing at the edge of my sight?

I started up the stairway, touching my feet onto the stonework with the stealth of a huntress. Light touch. Sharp awareness. I kept my arms out in front of me in case I ran into a wall in the darkness.

The stairs changed direction twice. I could hear singing again from below, muffled by the walls as if someone were trying to strangle the music. That didn't make the voices of the choir any less mesmerizing. I walked upward in the darkness. The passageway felt so distant from the rest of the world. Like a place between life and death. The fraction of time crammed between one heartbeat and the next.

At last a long stream of light poured through the dark. A door left wide open at the top of the stairs. I stopped to let my eyes adjust once again then moved forward.

The door led into a small room with a single window. A pair of doves nestled on the windowsill outside with their backs to the glass, overlooking the rooftop of the cathedral as if it were a balcony The walls of the room were lined with shelves filled with volume after volume of thick leather bound books. It smelled of leather and parchment and ink and dust. It smelled like Papa's study.

Only Papa had never chained his books to the shelves. Long black chains hung from the front covers of most of the larger volumes, as if to hold their knowledge captive. I shuddered to see the damage the incisions had done but at least they had had the sense not to chain them at the bindings.

The noble girl stood next to a shelf with a black leather bound volume in her hand. It was chained. She turned. Her gold silk gown rustled. She had gold eyes and gold hair to match, combed neatly into a net behind her ears. She stared at me with surprise and . . . something else.

"You are Princess Snow." She said at last. "The Huntsman's Apprentice. My betrothed is in love with you."

I blushed. This was Princess Ava then. Otto's betrothed. My mother's sister's daughter. My cousin. I opened my mouth to speak but she spoke first.

"Don't deny it. Anyone only has to hear him speak your name to know that it is true."

"I'm not a princess." I said. "Not anymore."

She tilted her head, watching me keenly. "You're Princess Rose's consort. That's close enough to being a princess yourself." She smiled. A sly, thin smile, brimming with secrets. "And you didn't bow when you realized who I was. At the core you are still royalty even if you have abdicated your kingdom." Her hand rested on the large black volume chained to the shelf. She stroked the binding lovingly, watching where my eyes had gone. "They look ominous don't they?" She had small, soft hands, untouched by work except for the tiny needle scars on her fingers. Once I had had hands like that. Now they were worn and rough from setting traps and chopping firewood.

"Why are they chained?" I asked. First the bears, and now the books. It seemed like everything in this castle was caged.

"For the same reason this whole library is hidden." Ava said.

"Because the books are valuable?"

"Because they are dangerous." She let go of the black volume and picked up another one next to it. Smaller. Sleeker. It wasn't chained. "I stole this one from the queen's chamber when she was ill. It was her most prized possession. She guarded it like a dragon guards its hoards of gold. I never would have got near it if she hadn't been so fogged with fever."

"The queen of the Southern Ridges. Your mother?" My heart pounded. My mother's older sister. The girl with freckles Otto had once been betrothed to.

Ava clutched the book in her hands. Her face clouded with the remnants of a story I knew nothing about. "Yes."

"What was she like?" I asked. It seemed odd that she would steal books from her own mother but then I had never had a mother myself. The closest had been Lucille. I shuddered.

Ava sighed, clutching the book tightly. "Regal. Clever. A charming face full of freckles. Otto loves to talk about my mother." She tapped her fingers over the cover of the book. Anxiously. As if trying to drum her thoughts out of her head. "He wishes I were her."

"They were friends." I said. "Before he was cursed."

"They were betrothed." She flashed me a harsh smile. "It seems my husband-to-be wishes he were marrying anyone but me."

I remembered Otto telling me about her mother what felt like a lifetime ago inside the hobgoblin's hovel. I hadn't realized she was my aunt back then. "He didn't love her. Not like that." I assured her.

"She loved him though. That's why she didn't come for the wedding. She said it would be too strange."

Nobles didn't marry for love. That was why I had chosen not to be one. A life without love hardly seemed worth living no matter how many feasts and velvet gowns your life was smothered in. Being royalty was like living in a cage. Rose was more precious to me than a thousand kingdoms.

Ava's sly, secretive smile returned to her lips, coyly, almost as if it knew it didn't belong there. That the moment was too solemn for smiles. She held out her hand. "Don't look so sad Cousin. It isn't your fault after all. It is high time I stopped feeling sorry for myself. Come. Choose a book and we will read it together." She winked. "Anything to escape the dullness of the bishop's sermon."

There were almost too many volumes to choose from. I pulled a dusty tome off the shelf and opened it. The script was difficult to make out. A messy inky scrawl in a language I didn't know. Probably the same language the singing had been in. Latin, my tutors had called it. A language for priests. For prayers and holy things. We had never had a priest at Papa's manor. Papa had always said we couldn't afford one. I put the book away.

My hand strayed to one of the chained books -the same black, leather bound volume Ava had been holding when I had entered the library. I picked it up. It was heavy. Hard to lift, especially with the thick iron chain pulling down on the cover. The links chinked against each other as I balanced the book in my hands and peeled it open. Dust rose up from the pages. I wheezed, then coughed. How long had it been since this book had been opened?

Divination

The first page read in ornate, neatly inked letters.

Ava peered over my shoulder. Her chin was almost close enough to touch my chin. "Do you want to know your future, Snow?" She asked.

"No." I said with more vehemence than I expected. I slammed the book shut. Dust clouded into the air, collecting in my eyes and mouth. I coughed.

Ava sneezed. Then she laughed. "What are you afraid of?"

"Change." I glanced out the window. The two doves perched together on the ledge moved closer together for warmth. It was a rare moment of comfort for them in their short, hard lives. The world around them was so vast. So full of trials. Why experience the future a moment before I had to?

Ava slid the book out of my hands. "Let's find something less heavy then. There was a charming book of love poems I found last week."

ROSE

Louisa brought in a platter of cheese and fruit with milk and pastries. I pulled myself up in bed and bit into a pastry, savoring the rich texture of baked apple and nut.

"Shall I get the drapes, Princess?"

I shook my head. "I'll get them." I set the pastry back on the tray and leapt out of bed. The long, thick pieces of fabric draped over the window slid away from the glass easily beneath my touch. Light streamed in in a thick, blinding avalanche. I squinted, shading my eyes with my hands until I could make out the intricate tracings of the towers and walls that filled the ward below. The towers seemed to reach into forever, smothered in carvings of animals and rose vines. The sky was bright but a cluster of clouds lurked in the distance. A storm edging its way toward us. It made the buildings seem even more majestic. Calm. Steadfast even against impending danger. "Snow, come look at . . ."

I turned toward the bed but Snow wasn't lying where I had tucked her away the night before. She must have woken earlier and left to explore the castle.

I stepped away from the window.

"Shall I help you dress, Princess?"

I turned toward Louisa, perplexed. Help me dress? I wasn't a child. Why would I need help with something as simple as dressing?

A moment later Louisa was struggling to pull a heavy velvet gown over my head while I held down a fragile silk shift beneath it. At last the tight, heavy gown slid into place. Louisa began lacing up the back. Her fingers worked quickly, weaving the ribbon in a complex pattern I couldn't see. When she had finally finished she ran a comb through my hair, pulling my curls up into an ornate arrangement on top of my head. My stomach rumbled. I eyed the tray of cheese and pastries longingly as the lonely bite of pastry swam around inside my belly. Did nobles always take this long to get dressed?

Louisa worked silently. Her lips pursed into a tight, serious line of concentration as she arranged each detail. Finally, she tugged the last strand of my hair into place. She stood back with a proud smile, admiring her creation. "There. The king said the red would suit you. I lengthened the hem myself. You look just like her."

I tilted my head curiously. "Like who?"

"Your mother." She winked. "She worked with me in the scullery when she was your age. A fiery girl. Always looking for trouble. But cunning enough to land herself a king in the end."

My mother. The scullery maid who had become queen.

"See for yourself." Louisa turned me in the direction of a long silver mirror. I stared. The tips of my curls hung neatly in an elegant frame around my face. The velvet gown spilled down to the floor in a long elegant shower. Gold embroidery traced my wrists and the hem of my bodice. Could that really be me? For a moment I thought I must be looking at another portrait of the vixen queen I had seen last night. I didn't look like Rose the spinner's apprentice or even the Red Witch of the wood. I looked like . . . like the princess everyone kept telling me I was.

I looked like my mother. I looked like I belonged here.

"Anything else I can do for you, princess?" Louisa asked.

I shook my head, still gazing, awestruck, at my reflection.

Louisa shuffled beside me. I heard the rattling of a tray and then the click of a door. I turned suddenly, realizing too late that she had taken my breakfast away with her.

I laughed. What did it matter? Another fine meal would be served soon. Today I was a princess. I wanted to enjoy it. I would play the part like a troubadour singing his tales.

I made my way through all three of our rooms and stepped out into the corridor, giddy with excitement. Beautiful things surrounded me. Ornate candlesticks. Brilliantly embroidered tapestries. Windows made of colored glass. Engraved weapons mounted on the wall. I glanced at the extravagances as I passed them, pattering my way down the corridor without stopping. It was as if my feet had already decided where I was going. I wove my way through the long narrow passages, never hesitating as I turned each corner. I moved as if in a dance, propelling myself forward with a graceful certainty I did not understand.

I glided my way up a long, twisted staircase and stopped. Suddenly. Certainly. This was it. Here. Behind this door. I had arrived.

I touched the latch on the door. My heart fluttered inside my breast, preparing myself for . . .

What? Why had my feet led me here as if I were performing some long forgotten dance learned in my childhood?

My childhood. Started inside this very castle.

My hand hovered over the brass latch. I breathed deep, trying in vain to calm the wild beating of my heart. I lifted the latch. The door clicked. Another flutter of excitement rippled through me. I pulled it open.

It was a private chamber like any of the other opulent rooms in the castle. Very much like the one Snow and I had slept in. Thick, embroidered curtains, tapestries and rugs covered the walls and floors to soften the cold of the stone walls. A fireplace stood in the corner. Velvet sofas filled the space. Only . . .

The bed was a child's bed. A crib, draped in gauzy white silk. Next to it was a spinning wheel with no spindle.

Gran's spinning wheel.

A memory flickered through my mind. The taste of wax in my mouth as I sampled a candlestick, perplexed that no one was there to stop me. The smell of smoke. The strangely terrified expression of a man with a sword as he stooped to pick me up.

My heart stood still. How could I remember? I couldn't have been a year old.

"This was our nursery."

I turned, startled by the sound of Otto's voice. I hadn't heard him come up behind me. "You scared me." I said.

"It was my nursery first, then yours." He continued. He pointed to a door behind the crib. "Nurse's room is back there."

Nurse. He meant Gran. My heart scurried like animals on the forest floor. Like kindling breaking apart into embers.

"I come here to think sometimes." Otto went on. "It soothes me. I'm not sure why Lucille never had the rooms changed when she took over the castle."

"Gran was her sister." I said. Perhaps there had been a lingering touch of softness in the queen's heart after all. Or perhaps she couldn't be bothered. One hardly thought about the furniture when one was busy conquering new kingdoms. But I was only half listening to what Otto was saying.

Our nursery. I had been born here. In this castle. I inhaled slowly, overwhelmed by the reality of it. Otto had been telling me this since he had returned to human form but I hadn't understood him until now. I hadn't believed him. Not really.

I had been a princess. I had been celebrated. Loved.

This was my home.

I was grateful for my life with Greta. She had been a kind guardian if sometimes strict. But a memory -faint and almost unreal -of my mother's laugh drifted through my mind like crystal. Another memory of my father's big, strong hands as he scooped me up into his arms and lift me over his head.

That's all it was. A memory. A glimmer of my past that I had forgotten until now. The faintest remnant of the family Lucille had taken from me.

A drop of salt water crawled into my mouth and I realized I was crying. I wiped the tears away and turned to look at Otto. My brother. My family who had found me.

Otto had strode over to the window. He gazed out of the glass with a worried, pensive expression as if he were some great hero in a play.

I wiped the rest of the tears off my face with the back of my hand and moved to stand next to him. What was wrong with me? I never cried this easily.

The busyness in the ward below was a stark contrast to the quiet inside the nursery. Tiny people rushed back and forth with tiny tasks. Carrying water. Feeding chickens. Chopping wood. It all seemed futile from up here. The water would dry up. The chickens would be hungry again. The wood would burn. And yet they all scurried about in a mad rush as if the earth depended on their tasks.

There was a menagerie of statues in the center of the ward near the entrance to the keep. A lion. A fox. A wolf. A stallion. A stone mason stood amongst them chipping away at a new statue, almost finished. It was big and round and stood on thick hind legs. The statue's fur was carved from a pure, white alabaster but one look at it and I couldn't help but imagine it was a bright copper red as Otto's had been when he'd been a bear. The same as both our hair was now. The same as mother's had been.

"It's you." I said.

Otto blushed. "The court insisted on building it in my honor. It's a tradition. All the animals represent our family through the ages. They built a Lion for father and a fox for mother."

"I know." I said. I was growing used to knowing things without knowing how I knew them.

Otto grinned. A mischievous, childish grin. "I'll have them make something for you next. A songbird perhaps."

A slow smile crept across my lips. A statue made in my honor. I did not dislike the idea.

Otto pointed out past the castle grounds to a far off glen. "That's the glen I told you about. Where I used to hunt. That's where I kissed Ava's mother for the first time. I must have been thirteen. Maybe twelve. I want to take you there before the wedding -you and Snow."

My excitement drooped like a plucked flower. I didn't like that he was talking about kissing girls in places he wanted to take Snow but I wanted to see where he had hunted as a boy. I grinned at him mischievously. Almost teasing. "Why not now?"

He shook his head. "The kitchen lost another sack of flour this morning. I have to help the bailiff sniff out who took it or Sludge will have my head."

I laughed. "I thought the hobgoblins were your spies, not the other way around."

Otto chuckled. "Try telling that to them."

"The sacks of flour will still be missing when you get back." I said. "You can sniff out the culprit then."

He gave me a sideways glance. "Missing flour might not sound important but to the villagers it is. They worked hard to supply extra food this harvest for my wedding guests. Feeding a castle full of nobles is no simple matter and I must make a show of prosperity before my subjects." All the same I could see his resolve wavering.

I touched his arm. "Come Brother. We never got the chance to sneak off and find mischief together as children."

His mischievous, childish grin returned to his face. A moment later we were creeping our way through the corridors. We stepped lightly, taking care to stay out of sight of the pages and other courtiers. We pressed against a corner, letting a lord walk sleepily past in his green embroidered dressing gown.

"You are the king." I hissed after the lord had disappeared. "You could tell them you want to take the day off."

Otto shook his head. "There are certain expectations of a king. He must be present to serve his people. To look after his guests. Slipping away suddenly and without reason would be looked very poorly upon. Besides." He winked. "This is more fun."

Once outside the keep it was more difficult not to be seen. If we had been dressed simply we could easily have blended into the busy swarm of servants but the red velvet Louisa had dressed me in and Otto's gold shirt and cloak drew all eyes to us like flies to honey. We had to settle for rushing past quickly as if we were going somewhere important with no time to answer questions. We strode through the inner ward first then through the outer ward with silent, serious expressions. The servants would never think to question where their king was going. With any luck they would never mention it to the courtiers either. The only ones to block our paths were three hens escaped from the laying pens and we quickly stepped around them.

The crowd thinned in the outer ward until it disappeared entirely. At last we reached a small gate on the side of the wall. No one saw the king and his sister slip out into the fields surrounding the castle.

We walked more freely now that we were out of sight. Our steps were light and our arms swung at our sides. A few feet outside the gate was a stone archway. Thorns grew up over it, disappearing into the ground. The wall it had once been a part of had eroded. Probably years before Lucille had laid siege to the castle. The thought reminded me how old the building was. How long it had been a part of my family.

Family. The word felt so strange in my mind.

Next to the archway was a lump attached to a long pike. A stench wafted through the air, rank like a mildewed chamber pot, as we came nearer. Gnats and flies swarmed around our faces. We waved our hands, trying to swat them away.

"The devil." Otto said when we were near enough to see what the lump on top of the pike was.

A horse's head stared at us with its flesh half rotted away. Its hair and skin hung loose over hollowed jaws. Clumps of brown blood were crusted to the hacked edges of its neck. Maggots crawled in and out of its empty eye sockets.

Otto stopped. He stared at the horrific display. "That's a village ritual I haven't seen before. I've seen plenty of straw men and wax dolls but never an animal's head on a pole. I'll have to ask Alf what it means."

I stared at the horse's head. The carcass stared back. Eerie. Reeking. The stench was nauseating. I'd grown up in a village but I'd never seen anything like this either. Not even at the harvest bonfires where they burned their straw men and let their wax dolls melt.

We moved away from the moorland and toward the woods. The trees were tall here. Wide. The trunks crept up, almost stepping into the path as we walked. It was an old path. It had been there since the trees were young, maintained by the feet and hooves of hunters and their horses throughout the century. A strong wind rustled through the trees. It whistled past my ear. I shivered, then stopped, listening.

Had I heard . . .

I couldn't have. That part of me had stopped hearing years ago.

"What's wrong?" Otto asked.

I breathed deep and slow, absorbing the chill that lingered in the air. It seeped through me, burrowing into my core. Memories stared at me, frozen in time like a portrait on the wall. A light flickered inside me. A light I hadn't felt in years, defiant against the cold.

There it was again. Not the wind's voice, no. Another voice, tangled inside the wind. The whisper of someone else's core. Their magic swept away inside the strengthening gust of wind as it soared through the trees.

The gust grew stronger. A bite of cold pierced through me. The flame inside me flickered, hardly more than an ember. My magic. Loosened. Free at last. The air tangled through my hair, pulling it behind me. A leaf caught in my curls. Another stuck to my face. I held still, bracing myself against the ice cold push of the wind.

The call grew stronger. A low, mournful song rooted in my core. I felt it brush through the forest, roaring, tumbling, soaring. I flew with it, higher and higher into the sky. It swirled in a playful dance as I drifted with it through the feathers of a hawk, through beams of sunlight flirting with the sky. The flame in the my core laughed. It stretched and flickered, growing stronger.

Something struck my face. I blinked, settling my awareness back into my body. I pulled the item away. All at once the wind stopped. Both song and flame disappeared. I stared at the course, rank piece of wool in my hand.

"That's my hat."

A smudge faced boy stood in front of us with his hand held out, waiting for me to give him back his hat. I reached out to oblige but the wind picked up again along with the voice inside it and the hat pushed back into my face.

Otto laughed. "The wind appears to think otherwise."

The voice ebbed gently as the wind lessened. I clutched the piece of wool in my hand.

The boy sighed. He crossed his arms in front of his chest, reminding me of Trouble. "It's no use." He said. "She's not done with her hair yet."

My nose scrunched in confusion. What was he talking about? "Who isn't done with her hair?"

"Gerti." He rolled his eyes. "She herds the geese with me. Every day she says a little rhyme. The wind blows my hat away and she combs her hair while I chase after it."

"Magic." Otto said.

The boy scowled. "Black magic. You should have her dismissed. You don't want witches herding your geese."

"I'm a witch." I said before I realized I'd said it. It wasn't true of course - not anymore- but I didn't want this poor girl to be dismissed for using magic. Even if it was a strange way to use it.

Otto raised his eyebrows. "Witchcraft is not a crime."

"Stealing people's hats is."

"She returns it to you by the end of the day." I pointed out.

The boy glared.

I lifted the hat and tried once again to hand it to him. This time the air stood still. He touched the limp piece of wool and lifted it cautiously out of my hand. I listened but couldn't hear anything inside the wind. The voice was gone.

"There." I said. "No harm done."

The voice was gone but I knew I hadn't imagined it. Magic grazing my soul once again. My heart pounded in my chest. My pulse rushed like a water mill. It had been so easy. As if my flame had never been gone at all.

The boy clutched his hat in his fist. He turned and scurried away through the trees.

It was a long walk to the glen. Otto told me about his hunts with father when he had been a boy as we walked. He told me how he had ridden in the king's saddle until he was old enough to ride for himself. How mother had insisted that she join them on their hunts, always the fastest rider. Always at the front of the chase.

"I hope I am a good king." He said. "I hope I make them proud."

It wasn't until we reached the glen that we realized neither of us had thought to bring food. Our bellies rumbled at each other until Otto took his sword and speared a fish in the stream. I gathered some kindling but Otto couldn't find his flint. I stared at the pile of firewood I had arranged, wondering if I could light it with my eyes the way I once had. My flame was still alive. The voice in the wind had brushed past it. Could I awaken it again? Could I use it?

At last Otto found his flint, hidden away inside his boot. He shrugged. "I don't use it except when I'm hunting. I forget sometimes where I put it."

We gutted the fish and cooked it. I looked down at my gown when we had finished, smothered in mud and fish guts. So much for playing the part of a princess. I didn't look much like a painting anymore unless it was a smudged one with colors running together.

"They really will think you're Mother now." Otto said. "She always came back from the hunts with another ruined gown. Our seamstresses were kept very busy."

I laughed. The thought was comforting. Perhaps Mother and Father would have been proud of me too.

It was well past dusk by the time we returned to the keep. I rushed upstairs and allowed Louisa to change me into a fresh gown, wash my face, and pull the leaves out of my hair.

"Where is Snow?" I asked as she placed a jeweled pin into the fresh arrangement in my hair.

Louisa raised an eyebrow. "I haven't seen her today. She must have dressed herself." She pulled one final curl into place and pinned it. She smiled, taking a step back to admire her work. "It's nice to have a girl to dress again. It feels like the old days, before Lucille. Every night was a feasting night back then." Her eyes clouded with memory. What had it been like for her, serving under Lucille? Greta had done the same for a time but she had never spoken about it. Almost as if she'd wanted to pretend it had never happened.

I heard the music long before I reached the great hall. Bright, charming ripples frolicked inside my ears, getting louder as I neared. A girl in gold silk fell in step beside me as I began the descent down the stairs. Pearls dripped from her ears and draped around her throat. She smiled a warm charming smile.

"Red curls. Gold eyes. A smile like fire. I've seen your portrait all over the castle walls long before you arrived." She said. "You must be Princess Rose. The Red Witch."

"Yes." I returned her smile before I realized that I hadn't told her I wasn't a witch anymore.

We stepped down into the hall. She took my hand. "I'm Princess Ava, Otto's betrothed. He speaks so highly of you."

I stopped, only half listening as I looked up at the windows reaching all the way to the top story of the keep. The ceiling stretched high like a cavern, higher than any tree canopy I'd ever stood beneath. The arches were engraved with thorns and roses and long twisting vines. Candelabras lined the walls, flickering like a hundred twinkling stars. Courtiers whisked back and forth in fine silks and velvet, tittering and laughing to each other as if nothing in the world mattered except the pleasure of each other's company.

"Princess Rose, I presume."

I turned. A tall gray haired courtier extended his hand. I took it, allowing him to graze his lips across my fingers.

"Asher. Merchant and land holder. It is a pleasure."

"Asher, you mustn't hog the Red Witch all to yourself." A charming, lazy voice drawled. I turned again. A muscular man flashed me a smile almost as lazy as his voice. He wore a green coat, crawling with intricate embroidery. My head danced, trying to decipher what the patterns were. He held out his hand. "Lord Bastian. You must forgive us if we crowd around you like flies to honey. You are a bit of a legend, you know."

"Why?" I asked. "Because I killed Lucille? It was mostly Snow who did that."

Lord Bastian eyed me up and down with the expression a spinner would examine another spinner's thread. "I didn't believe them when they said you looked just like Dehlia but you could have walked straight out of one of her portraits. Especially in that gown. Velvet suits you, my dear."

"Thank you." I turned around, looking for Ava but she had already faded into the lively mesh of courtiers.

Lord Bastian winked. "You will eclipse even the king's bride-to-be tonight."

"That doesn't take much." Asher muttered.

Lord Bastian rolled his eyes. He leaned forward with a conspirator's twinkle in his eye. "Asher still hopes that King Otto will change his mind and wait another two years until his daughter, Mirah, is old enough to wed. A futile hope but he refuses to give it up."

"It's not futile." Asher insisted. "My wares and landholdings are worth more than the tiny little kingdom of the Southern Ridges. Otto would gain riches and my daughter would have a title to give my grandchildren. It would be a profitable marriage for both sides."

"Pish posh. Otto already owns all your land before you do. He's the king."

Asher lifted a finger and pointed it at Bastian's embroidered breast. "I still have a better chance at persuading him to give up the marriage than you do. He's a king. He needs heirs."

Lord Bastian waved a hand. "I don't have to persuade him to give up anything. All I have to do is hope he doesn't insist on being faithful to Ava. Few men are faithful to their wives, especially once they've encountered my devilish grin." He flashed a demonstration.

Asher rolled his eyes, exaggerating how unimpressed he was by the grin.

"Don't look so disapproving Princess." Bastian laughed. " Any half-wit can see that the bride and groom share no affection for one another. Would you resign your brother to a life without love? Someone has to appreciate those quiet, bear-like eyes of his the way he deserves."

"Affection comes later." Asher said. "It's making a sensible match that matters, especially to a king."

"Everyone knows he's really in love with the Hunter's Apprentice." Bastian said. "Is that her?"

I followed his gaze to the bottom of the staircase. Snow made her way toward me. She wore a purple velvet gown with simple lacings on the sides. Her black hair was loose and long around her ears and her feet were completely bare. She seemed entirely unconscious of the stares that followed her as she made her way through the hall. Eyes watched as her skirt swished with the sway of her hips. Her movements were smooth and controlled with the precision of the huntress she was. Her serious eyes and half smile were more beautiful than all the jewels and silk drifting and tittering around her. Her cheeks turned a sweet shade of pink, shadowed by the bruise still on her face, as she came nearer with her gaze locked onto mine.

"Is it true that she killed a were with her bare hands?" Bastian whispered in my ear.

I laughed. "Of course not."

Snow stopped in front of me. "What?" She asked, curious about my laughter.

I kissed her temple. "Velvet suits you."

She blinked at me in realization. "Oh." She said. "You're wearing velvet too, aren't you? And jewels. Is that amethyst? It's lovely."

My lips twisted into a half smile to match hers. "You didn't notice until now?"

"No." She said. "I was looking at you."

"Barefoot." Bastian said, this time loud enough for her to hear. "Is that the fashion in the south or are you trying to show off your barbaric woodland nature?"

Snow's cheeks flushed again. She looked down at her feet. "I fell asleep in the library. It was dark when I woke and I couldn't find where I kicked off my slippers in my sleep."

Bastian sighed a martyr's sigh. "What a disappointingly dull explanation."

"If you will excuse me." Asher bowed his head. "I must see to my daughter." He made his way across the room to stand next to a dark haired girl barely old enough to be allowed to dine with the courtiers. Fourteen. Perhaps fifteen. She had wide, eager eyes and a shy smile as she gazed at the splendor that surrounded her.

The musicians began a new melody. A soft tinkering like rain against glass that echoed through the hall. I looked across the swirl of courtiers to see one of Trouble's brothers fingering a pipe with the other musicians. His long, thin hobgoblin fingers moved expertly up and down with the lively tune.

Bastian cleared his throat. "You must excuse me as well." He winked and drifted into the crowd to find a young lord to dance with.

I turned back to Snow, incredulous. "They seem to be afraid of you."

She looked puzzled. "Why?"

As if she didn't know how strikingly fierce she was. I took her hand. "Let's dance." I wasn't about to let all that practice go to waste.

Snow hesitated. She glanced at the courtiers around her as if they might gobble her up. Perhaps she hadn't been as unconscious of their stares as she'd seemed. She looked like she might be sick.

I squeezed her hand tight, holding her gaze so that she had to look at me and not the courtiers whirling past us in time to the music. They glided across the room like the clouds in my dream, their feet never seeming to touch the ground. "Remember our bonfire?" I asked. "The first time you showed me how to dance. When the animals came."

Snow nodded.

"That was the night I realized I was a witch." The magic from the wind earlier that day echoed inside me as I realized I had almost said "am". I placed one of my hands on her shoulder and pulled hers in to touch my waist on the other side. We were almost close enough for our breasts to touch. "This is no different than that."

I moved my foot. She mirrored the movement with her bare toe pointed elegantly beneath her skirt. I moved my other foot and she followed. Her eyes locked on mine. The splendor of the great hall disappeared in their star-filled glint, deep and perilous like the night sky.

The flawless movements of the other courtiers melted away beneath the warmth of her touch. How did it still make my heart race like a hunted deer? Even the lull of the music gave way to the delicious movements of her body as we swayed together. I spun her around then pulled her back in, even closer this time. All that existed was me and her and the seductive pulse of our movements as we skirted in one direction, then the other. She spun me then I spun her then we both spun, always returning to the safety of each other's arms. The moment seemed to last forever. It seemed to be gone in a blink. Suddenly the music stopped. We stood, grinning at each other as we tried to catch our breath.

"You danced beautifully." I started at the sound of Otto's voice. The crowded press of the courtiers' eyes slowly faded back into my awareness. They had grown silent and still as they stopped to watch us dance.

I turned toward Otto. He stood behind me with Ava on his arm. He grinned. "You were born to be a courtier."

I preened at the praise and squeezed Snow's hand. The music picked up again, this time softer, bubbling like warm soup in a cauldron. Happy chatter crescendoed around us once more as the light from the candelabras flickered against the ornate carvings on the walls and ceilings. Every sensation was overwhelmingly beautiful. How had I ever been afraid to come here?

"Can we really live here with you?" I asked Otto. "Forever?"

"Of course." He said. "This is your home. You belong here. Both of you."

SNOW

Belong here? That was ridiculous. Rose belonged in the wood with the pines and the squirrels and our harvest bonfires. We both did. I opened my mouth but no sound came out.

Ava touched my arm. "Snow and I found the most charming love poems in the library today, didn't we, Cousin?"

I blinked. Suddenly everyone was staring at me. Rose. Otto. Ava. A lady with a stern matronly gaze who had joined the circle. I tried not to sink into the floor. Their gazes were expectant. Scrutinizing. It took me a moment to shake off the shock of Rose's request. I stammered out the best description of the poems I could manage. My voice was hardly audible even to me.

Rose laughed. "Trust Snow to be at a castle this grand and spend the whole day in the library. Do you know what I saw today?" She told of her own adventures discovering a horse's head on a spike and ruining her gown gutting a fish. Her face lit up as she told the tale, describing every detail as if she were a troubadour who had practiced it for weeks. The others listened with rapt attention, absorbing every syllable as if it were a sweet.

"You did this all on your own?" The stern matronly lady asked. "That's rather bold of you all alone in a strange place."

Rose glanced at Otto. He cleared his throat. "Shall we make our way to the dining hall?"

We did as he suggested and filtered through the large oak door at the end of the hall and took our places at the table. I sat across from Rose with the stern matronly lady seated on one side and the lord in green embroidery who had asked me about my feet seated on the other. The lady bent her head close to mine. She lowered her voice.

"Is it true that Hans the Hunter kept a necklace made from the teeth of the children he killed?"

I turned toward her, horrified. "Of course not." I snapped. "Don't ask stupid questions," As if Hans had been proud of the children he had killed. As if he had enjoyed it.

She turned away, avoiding my eyes as the servant brought in the first course. A creamy bay leaf soup with butterkase cheese, rye and a soft braided bread someone called challah. The lady spoke to the lady on the other side of her in a hushed voice. I caught the word 'killer' as she snuck a glance in my direction. I resisted the urge to get up and leave and concentrated on my soup.

"What do you think of this cold weather?" The lord with the green embroidery asked. He had a mischievous, conspirator's glint in his eyes.

"It's cold." I answered.

"Yes." He winked. "Usual for this time of year, don't you think?"

I stared at him, feeling as if he expected me to say more. "Yes." I said at last. "I imagine it is."

The twinkle in his eye shriveled. "Have you always been this sullen and drab, my dear, or is that something the Hunter taught you?"

"I don't know." I answered.

He turned and spoke to the lord on the other side of him.

Fish and onions with roasted vegetables were served next. Conversation cascaded around me. I watched Rose across from me as she laughed and chatted with her dinner companions. Her hair and eyes glinted like fire in the light from the candles. Her delicate pointed nose reminded me for a moment of a fox, sleek and clever. Her laughter tinkled like crystal. "Please tell me, Bastian." She pleaded of the lord in green embroidery. "What happened when you realized your new clothes were invisible?."

The lord laughed. "What happened? Nothing at all. Except that I took my gold back from the tailor and spending whole days with no clothes on became the fashion for the rest of the summer. I never told them that I had thought I was clothed the whole day. They thought it was all a great lark."

Rose laughed again, loud and strong like a gust of wind.

Wine flowed and the conversation got livelier and livelier. I listened, nibbling quietly at Sludge's creations. He had done a masterful job. The fish and onions had fennel in them. I wondered if I could make them with nutmeg.

Next was a roasted swan with gravy as rich as kings. Eyes darting in my direction as I ate then pulled back as if my glance alone might turn them into one of my hunted carcasses. I looked over at Ava sitting next to Otto, hoping for a friendly glance. She was locked in conversation with a tall man with a long beard. Otto was speaking with a young dark haired girl seated on the other side of him. I tried to remember if he had once glanced at his betrothed the entire evening. I couldn't recall that he had. Not even when she had been dutifully clutching his arm in the great hall.

Finally dessert was served. Cherry strudel and custard followed by hot roasted chestnuts. The chatter quieted slowly as the meal came to an end. A juggler was ushered into the dining hall. He juggled apples first, then knives, slicing the apples with them in midair. I watched the way he flicked his wrists to get the knives in the air. Precise and quick. It was a technique I had never seen before.

When the juggler had finished the plates were cleared away. Some of the courtiers drifted off to bed while others returned to the great hall, chatting and laughing as if the night were still young. Rose went with them, pulled along by Bastian and the stern faced lady. The room quieted slowly. I lingered, savoring the stillness the last courtiers drifted out.

A soft chirping touched my ears. I stood and turned toward the sound. An ornate iron cage stood in the corner of the room. Four song birds sat inside, singing relentlessly with the power of their tiny breasts. I hadn't noticed them in all the commotion.

Another cage.

"They're Ava's." Otto said, coming up beside me. The room was empty now except for the two of us. "She said they reminded her of home."

"Are they southern birds?" I asked.

"Yes." Otto's voice was quiet. Soft.

"They're beautiful." They reminded me of our home in the woods but it saddened me to see them in a cage. "Rose loves it here." I said.

"You don't?" Otto sounded surprised.

I shook my head. I didn't hate it. Not exactly. But I missed the intimacy of our cottage. The wild earthiness of the wood. Unpleasant memories seemed to till themselves up at every corner here.

"Rose belongs here." Otto said. "You must see that."

"She belongs in the woodland." I said. "She belongs with me." But I couldn't deny there was truth in his words. She had blended so seamlessly with the other courtiers at dinner, glowing with the energy of their chatter.

She wanted to stay.

I tilted my head, curious. "Why do you not speak with your bride?" I asked.

Otto sighed. "I've tried. I really have. She's pretty. She's polite. She always laughs when she's supposed to. She's absolutely nothing like her mother. She was such an earthy girl. She always laughed at the wrong times. It made her much easier to talk to."

"Ava thinks you're in love with her mother."

Otto raised his eyebrows. He looked straight at me. "You know very well that that's not who I am in love with."

I tried not to blush

"You said it yourself." Otto's gaze was as unguarded as it was unyielding. "Kings and queens do not marry for love. The Southern Ridges are recognizing my rule by sending me their daughter. It is the best union I could have hoped for. Lucille weakened my family's name with her raids and violence. This marriage will strengthen it again."

I glanced again at the birds in the cage. Trapped together out of necessity whether they would or no. It was a tragic fate for anyone.

Otto and I turned back toward the great hall. The birds began to sing again as we drifted slowly across the room, calling after us with a sweet mournful call.

"I need to tell you something." I said. "I went to the kitchen today to visit Sludge and . . ."

An avalanche of chatter met us in the great hall. There was no more dancing but the wine from dinner had made everyone quite merry. Laughter echoed through the room as Otto and I stepped inside. A man strode through the tittering crowd toward Otto with thick forester's boots.

I stiffened. My whole body felt queasy as I remembered the bear and bear cub from my visit to the kitchen. The way he had spoken to the Ellie. The way he had been looking at Rose when we'd seen him in the forest. Sludge's fine feast gurgled in my belly, threatening to come to the surface.

Alf stopped when he reached us. He kneeled.

"Rise." Otto said. "What brings you into my hall tonight?" It was no common thing for a forester to enter the great hall during a feast. The chatter began to quiet around us.

Alf rose roughly to his feet. "A wedding gift for you, my king." He stepped aside, flourishing his arm toward the door. The crowd parted slowly.

The bear entered on his hind legs, towering over the crowd in a big furry shadow. His master shuffled in beside him, holding him up with the hooked stick on the ring in his nose. A gasp fluttered its way through the crowd, followed by a deep, still hush. The music stopped.

They reached the center of the hall. The master pulled the hook out of the bear's ring and stepped back. He pulled a pipe out from under his cloak and began to play.

It was a lively tune, flitting about the room, bright and brisk. The bear shuffled back and forth on his hind legs in time with the sweet, quick sounds. The courtiers began to cheer.

The bear danced. His eyes were fogged with fear and defeat as his paws rushed to keep up with the music. He moaned in pain but his feet did not stop moving, spurred forward by the memory of red hot coals when he was a cub.

Red hot coals like hot iron shoes. I looked at Otto. Surely he did not approve of this cruelty? He had been a bear himself under Lucille's curse.

"Stop this." I said.

The music kept playing. The bear kept dancing. My eyes darted through the hall, looking for Alf but he had disappeared into the crowd.

"This is cruel." I said, louder this time.

A handful of courtiers turned to look at me with a sneer in their eyes. The bear made some steps to the side. The courtiers laughed.

"Stop." This time I shouted.

Otto touched my arm. "Quiet." He hissed.

The master played his pipe. The bear shuffled his feet.

I turned toward Otto. My body shook with fury. "Don't you realize how that poor animal has been trained?"

Ott's grip tightened on my arm. "I remember." He hissed. "It is impolite for a king to refuse a gift in public. Especially from a subject who has so much less than me. Such an insult is not easily forgotten. I need my people to see me as magnanimous and generous, not cheerless and unaccepting. They need to trust me. If I deny the court their entertainment because it brings back painful memories I am serving myself, not them."

Painful memories? Had he been forced to dance as a bear before he had found me and Rose? He shuddered slightly. My tone softened. "The animal is in pain."

Otto nodded. "When the dance is over I will pay the bear master what taking away his livelihood is worth and release the bear into the forest."

"He won't know how to hunt."

"Snow" His voice was terse and worried, almost a growl. He glanced around us. Many of the courtiers had drawn their eyes away from the hypnotic sway of the bear's movements to watch us whispering. "There is another place for this conversation."

I caught Ava's eye, watching us from across the room. I blushed, realizing what she must have thought of my lengthy hushed conversation with her betrothed. His hand was still on my arm. I pulled it away. "There's something else." I said. "Your forester. Alf. He used to work for Lucille."

"I know." Otto said.

"What?" My jaw hung slack with shock. How could he know? Surely if he knew he would have dismissed the forester.

Or locked him up.

The music stopped. The hall erupted with applause. Otto stepped forward, clapping along with his courtiers. "Wonderful." He said. "Thank you for the magnificent gift. It will keep my marriage alive with music and dance. My page will tell you where to keep him." He whispered something quickly to a page who scurried after the bear and his master.

I looked around the room for Alf as the bear, master, and page stepped out into the night but he was nowhere to be seen.

The corridors were quiet when Rose and I at last began making our way back to our chambers. Some of the torches had gone out. I shivered in the darkness, looking forward to the warmth of our bed. My bare feet felt cold against the stone floor. Rose's slippers clicked gently beside me. She looked glorious in her velvet gown and carefully arranged hair. Just like a painting.

"Rose." I said.

She turned toward me. Sleek. Elegant.

What did I tell her? That I hated seeing her dressed up like a copy of her mother? That the noise and chatter of the feast had left me drained and craving her touch? That I missed home.

A gasp sounded in the darkness up ahead. Shadows moved. Murmurs. Tense voices, hardly audible. We turned toward the sound. I quickened my pace, moving closer until I could make out what they were saying.

"Don't be so coy, little darling. You're only a merchant's daughter. Nothing to act so grand about."

A larger shadow was looming over a smaller one. I could barely make them out in the dim flicker of torchlight. The smaller shadow backed away. The larger one reached out and grasped it fast, pulling it close.

I reached for where my knife should have been but all I grasped was a hand full of velvet. Rose caught up beside me. She gasped.

"And you are only a forester." A third shadow joined the other two. Ava's silhouette stood, sleek and commanding. "Let the child go and do not think that Asher will not hear of how you have treated his daughter."

Rose and I were close enough to see their faces now. Alf the forester had his hands gripped tight around the wrists of the young dark haired girl Otto had been speaking with. She pulled away from him, her eyes wide and frightened.

"King Otto will hear of it as well." I said, summoning my best lady of the manor voice. It held more threat than I'd expected, tainted with the ferocity of a huntress.

Something between annoyance and contempt flickered across Alf's face. I had expected Otto's name to inspire more fear. Was his hold over his subjects still so weak? I began to see why he relied so heavily on his union with Ava. Why he was so afraid of offending his courtiers.

Reluctantly Alf let go of the girl's wrists. She stepped back, cradling them in her palms. Alf squinted at Ava in the dark. "Who are you then, missy, to be tossing commands at a lowly forester like myself?"

"Her majesty, Princess Ava."

His squint deepened. "Are you now?"

Ava stared at him.

He cleared his throat. "There must be a misunderstanding. Mirah and I were just saying goodnight, weren't we darling?"

Mirah shook her head, still cradling her wrists.

"That's a dangerous game you are playing, forester." Ava said. "Accosting the king's guests."

Alf shrugged. "She's only a merchant's daughter."

"I remember what you said to me when you thought that I was only a woodland scavenger."

I turned toward Rose. Her chin was raised and her eyes were on fire but I could see her hands shaking. I wished more than ever that I had my knife. "What did he say to you?" I demanded.

Something almost like fear flickered across Alf's face for the first time. "It was all meant in good fun." He muttered. "Like you said. I didn't know who you were."

"Goodnight, Alf." Ava said coldly. Her voice echoed through the corridor, loud and powerful.

Alf glowered but at last he turned and walked away toward the stairs. We stood, rooted where we were until the click of his boots could no longer be heard.

I turned back toward Rose. "What did he say to you?"

She didn't answer.

Ava placed her hand on Mirah's shoulder. "Come, child. Let's get you to bed, then I will speak to your father."

Mirah's chambers were not far from ours. We walked with Ava and Mirah until they had closed the chamber doors behind them. I glanced at Rose as we continued through the corridor. Her hands had stopped shaking but it wasn't like her to be so quiet.

"We can leave as soon as the wedding is over." I said. To assure her. To assure myself.

She stopped just as we reached the chamber door. She placed her hand on the handle. Her brow scrunched in confusion. "Otto said we can stay."

"We don't have to." I said. "We can go home."

Rose turned toward me. Torchlight flickered across her face. She looked more than ever like her mother's painting. "This can be our home."

"No." I said.

She blinked. "You wanted to come. You wanted to see Otto."

"I did. Now I want to go home." I glanced behind us in the direction we had come. The direction Alf had been. "What did he say to you?" I asked for the third time.

Rose pushed the door open. "It's not important."

"It is." I insisted, staying where I was in the corridor. A surge of anger rose through me. "Why do you want to stay in a place that allows brutes like him to roam free? He was one of Lucille's men, Rose. I remember him."

"So do I." Rose said calmly. "Hans was one of Lucille's men, Snow."

"That's different." I snapped. "Hans wasn't filth. Why are you defending him?"

"I'm not defending Alf. I'm defending Otto. "My brother. He is not responsible for everything his servants do."

"He didn't have to let the bear dance." I said. The cruelty of it still made my stomach churn. ""We can't stay here."

"Because of a bear?"

"Because it's not our home." It was a tomb of finery where cruel men walked free and bears were made to dance in the halls. Even the books were chained. Rose had no idea how lonely being royalty really was or how much strain it was always having everybody's eyes on you. Always having to say the right thing and put your duty to your people before yourself. Before those you loved most. It was a cage.

Rose was silent for a moment. "My mother lived here, Snow." She said. "I belong here. Don't you love the music? The tapestries? The painting? All the rich foods?"

"No." I said. "I love our cottage. I love the smell of yeast in the morning when I make our bread. I love chopping wood in the quiet of dusk. You belong in the woodland, Rose. You've always belonged there."

Rose lifted her chin in the shadows. Her voice flared with anger. "You think I'm not good enough for a castle."

"That's not what I said."

"It's what you meant though. I'm just as much a princess as you are, Snow. More, because I didn't forfeit my kingdom. All this time I thought you forfeited it for me, but you didn't did you? You never wanted to be royalty. I was only an excuse for you to run away from your responsibilities."

It was true. I had been more than pleased to give up my title to live with her in the woods. The only place I had ever really been happy.

But I loved her. She had to know that. I would do anything for her.

"I won't stay here." I said and followed her into our chambers.

I woke to a screeching sound like I had only ever heard inside my own nightmares. I opened my eyes and shot up in bed. Rose stirred beside me, still asleep. I raised my hand to wake her then stopped. We had gone to sleep without mending our argument. She might not thank me for waking her. I rolled the blankets off my legs and pulled my knife out from underneath my pillow. It felt good to have it rested in the curve of my palm once again. I felt like myself. I felt safe.

The corridor was dark as pitch. Every last torch had been put out for the night. I gripped my knife tight in my fist, moving slowly in the darkness. The shadows of Rose's ancestors stared at me from the paintings on the walls with accusing glares. I shuddered. It was I who had stolen their daughter from them. I who had stopped her from claiming her birthright.

I shook the thought away, listening for the scream again but all was silent. Had I imagined it the way I had imagined the wolf in the mountains?

But I had not imagined the wolf even if it had seemed to disappear with the light of day. I had heard it, howling like a ghost into the night. I had seen its eyes, yellow in the darkness.

I shivered as my bare feet pressed against the stone floor. The scream had come from this direction. I was sure of it.

A few more steps. More silence. More darkness.

I turned a corner.

A candle flickered. Feet shuffled.

Then I saw her.

She stood at the end of the corridor. Wax from the candle in her hand dripped over her fingers and down onto the rug beneath her feet. She had her other hand clamped over her mouth as if to push the scream back into her mouth.

Mirah.

I quickened my pace. My toe hit something in the dark just as I reached her. I stopped, close enough to touch her shoulder with my hand.

A chill crept over me that had nothing to do with the drafty corridor. My toe pressed against flesh. It was still warm but . . . something was missing. The thing that distinguished an animal from a carcass. I looked down.

The body was little more than a long gray lump in the darkness. A thick inky shadow darker than the other shadows. Mirah's candle cast just enough light that I could make out the plain green and brown tunic of a forester.

I looked up at Mirah. Her mud colored eyes were wide, her face pale in the faint flicker of the candlelight. Her hand covered her whole chin.

"What happened?" I asked.

Mirah peeled her hand away from her mouth. "I don't know." She said. "I came out to fetch a fresh chamber pot and he was here."

I snatched the candle from her. The wax scalded my fingers as it poured over my hand but I ignored it. With the candle held over his face, I could see the corpse's features more clearly.

"Alf." I said, confirming what I had already known. His shirt was ripped open at the chest beneath his tunic, soaked in blood so fresh that it hadn't even turned brown yet. It gushed from a deep hole in the side of his neck - or was it a gash? From a knife perhaps. Or a spear. It was neater than any battle wound I'd ever seen. Clean. Precise. He had not been given time to defend himself. His thick, square jaw hung slack and stupid. His eyes bulged like a frog's.

I held up the candle to get a better look at Mirah. The thin fabric of her white night shift draped against her slight form. There were no signs of blood splatters. "What happened?" I asked again.

She shook her head. "I don't know." Her voice was steadier this time. She had stopped trembling.

Wax dripped from the candle down onto the corpse. I wasn't sorry he was dead. If anyone deserved a violent death it was him but I would hang before I saw Mirah tried for his murder.

Even if she had killed him.

The candle was little more than a stub now. The flame flickered weakly in the darkness. A draft poured in through a window I couldn't see. The candle went out. Mirah gasped. I gripped the hilt of my knife.

"If anyone else saw you standing over a dead body with a knife in your hand they might make assumptions Not-Princess Snow."

Ava's voice. Where had she come from so suddenly?

She touched my hand lightly in the dark. "Remember, you are a stranger here, Snow. The court knows nothing of you except that you are the Huntsman's Apprentice. A trained killer."

"A hunter." I corrected her but the argument tasted futile in my mouth. I shuddered, remembering all the murmurs and unfriendly glances from dinner.

"Mirah, child." Ava said. "He was already dead when you opened the door, was he not?"

"He was."

"Go to bed. The court will find him in the morning. Act as shocked as anyone else. Tell no one we were here."

Mirah hesitated but obeyed. She shifted away in the darkness. Her chamber door clicked close behind her.

"Quickly." Ava held out her hand. "Give me your knife and the candle. We must get rid of them."

"The knife is clean." I protested.

"It won't matter. The Huntsman was known to lick the blood off his blade when he had nothing to clean it with."

I shuddered. It might be true. Hans was nothing if not practical. I felt the weight of my knife's silver hilt in my palm. Hans had given it to me. It was all I had left of his memory apart from the skills he had taught me and the life he had sacrificed his for.

"You can come back for it." Ava promised. "You can't be seen wandering the corridors with a weapon tonight." She snatched the candle stub out of my hand. She reached for the knife but I pulled it back. "Please Snow. Do not think Otto's love for you will save you. He knows his duty to his people. He will uphold the law."

I shuddered thinking of the bear he let dance. How tight his grip had been. *I remember* he had said and yet he had let the animal dance for his court.

Grudgingly I allowed Ava to take the knife as well. She strode toward the draft sifting past us in the corridor and tossed both objects out the window. "Now." She said. "Lets get that wax off your fingers."

Ava led me through the corridors. We moved without a sound, cutting through the darkness like ghosts. The castle was silent except for low murmurs coming from a nearby chamber. Lovers saying a late night farewell. The voices were followed by footsteps, then the faint glow of a candle.

Ava stopped. She tugged at my wrist and we stepped around the corner, pressing our backs against the wall.

The footsteps brought with it a long shadow followed by the long, brisk strides of the lord from dinner. Bastian. He wore a loose embroidered dressing gown that did nothing to cover the hairs on his naked chest. He whistled softly as he approached.

He stopped when he reached the turn, hesitating as if he couldn't remember which way to go. He pointed one direction, then the other, mouthing to himself under his breath. The light from his candle was blinding. Ava and I pushed ourselves flatter against the wall. I struggled to keep my breathing silent. My heart pounded inside my chest, sounding like a drum in my ear.

At last he moved on, striding in his original direction. He resumed his whistling. The light from his candle drifted away slowly.

Ava pulled me through the corridor once again. We moved more quickly this time, striding through corridor after corridor in the dark. At last we stopped in front of a chamber and slipped inside.

Ava closed the door quietly behind us. She leaned with her back against it, breathing heavily. A fire flickered from across the room and I could see her clearly for the first time since she'd found me in the corridor. She was dressed in a silver dressing gown with her gold hair loose around her ears. Her breasts rose and fell with the the fatigued rhythm of her breath. She lifted her finger over her mouth to signal quiet. "Otto's chambers are across the hall. You're lucky I couldn't sleep tonight and fancied a walk to the library. Lord Bastian would have found you standing over Alf's body with that knife."

"My God." A muffled cry erupted from down the corridor. Bastian stumbling upon the body. "Murder! Murder!" He ran through the halls, sounding the alarm. "Murder! Murder!"

Ava raised her eyebrows at the proof of her words. She reached for my hand. "Let's get that wax off your fingers. I saw it drip on his face. Then we can join the throng of shocked courtiers gawking to see what happened."

I let her lead me to the fire. She dipped a cloth into a basin of water and rubbed it against my fingers. It seemed foolish to hide evidence of a murder I didn't commit. The more I tried to hide the more guilty I would look if I were found out. "How do you know I didn't kill him?" I asked. She was so certain that the court wouldn't believe my innocence. What proof did she have of it herself?

Ava rubbed furiously at my fingers. Bits of skin came off with the wax, made tender by the burns. I bit my lip, wincing at the pain.

"Because I know who did." Ava answered. "I told Asher that Alf had been accosting his daughter."

"You think it was Mirah's father?"

The last bit of wax fell off my fingers. Ava threw them into the fire. "Who else? Alf was killed outside his daughter's bedchamber. I shudder to think of what would have happened if I hadn't warned him but that may not save him from the noose."

"You told Otto too." I said, puzzled. "Why did he do nothing?" A flush of anger rushed to my face. Was accosting young girls at night another thing he turned a blind eye to in order to appear magnanimous before his subjects?

Ava sighed. "I do not know. Otto is cautious. Too cautious. Perhaps he did not believe me. Perhaps he did not think it was important. Perhaps his rule is still too weak to risk shaming one of his strongest fighters but I'm not sorry the man is dead."

"Neither am I." I said, remembering the way Alf had been looking at Rose when Trouble and I had found them together in the woods. What had he said to her?

A pounding of footsteps clamored through the corridor, followed by shouts and excited voices. The guards responding to Bastian's cries. I glanced at the door.

"Let us wait another moment." Ava said. "Until the other courtiers begin peeking their heads out."

I flexed my hand. The skin stung when I moved it. The burn was starting to blister where the skin hadn't already been torn off. "Do you always take walks to the library in the middle of the night?" I asked. It was a strange habit for a princess.

Ava smiled coyly. She swept away from the fireplace and picked a long, thin glass bottle off the table. The crystal glimmered in the firelight, darkened by the red liquid sloshing inside. "More frequently than you would think." She pulled a stopper off the top of the bottle and poured the liquid into two matching goblets. "It's the only place I can think, really. Even in my own chamber my handmaid is always lurking. She's asleep now, thankfully. The constant movement of castle life is exhausting. Sometimes I almost miss -" She placed the stopper back in the bottle and set it down with a contemplative expression on her face. "You look so much like your mother."

My brow wrinkled. "You couldn't have been a year when she left to marry Papa."

"I wasn't born yet but our halls in the south are full of portraits of the royal family. Opal had the same small nose and dark hair as you do, although her lips were not as red and her skin was not as pale. Did you know she was schooled in magic?"

I blinked. My mother was a witch like Rose?

"She was a shade." Ava whisked away from the table. She knelt behind a chaise lounge. Her voice carried from behind the white velvet pillows as she rummaged for something on the ground. "The royal family in the south have guarded the art of shade magic for generations. It's a dangerous thing to let fall into the wrong hands. "

As was any magic. I thought of Lucille and all the lives she had destroyed. Had Papa known that both his wives were witches?

Ava popped back up like a shadow puppet from behind the chaise lounge. In her hand was a book. The same little volume she had been clutching when I'd first met her. The one she said she had stolen from her mother. She held it out to me.

I stepped forward and took it. Curious, I peeled it open. The words were hard to make out in the dim light.

Eyna was burned for witchcraft in the year of our lord 304 but that was not the end of the strange illnesses that had swept through the Southern Ridges. She had already passed the art along to several apprentice shades who began to refine it into a precise discipline far superior to the wild, untamable arts of witches. It soon became apparent that this was a different, more powerful kind of magic. One that could force others to act against their will and against their nature.

Fascinated, I found another page.

These three drops of blood, howsoever they are obtained, are what will allow a shade to control their blood child. Every command will be obeyed without question, regardless of their will. Once made, a binding cannot be broken. Not even by the shade who made it.

I looked up, horrified. "My mother controlled people with their blood?"

Ava shook her head. Her gold skirts swished in the flicker of firelight as she made her way back across the room. "That's an ancient practice. Like burning witches. No one has done it for generations. Even if our consciences would allow us to it is too risky. Blood children dislike having their will taken from them. They always find ways to turn against you, obeying your words but not your intention, twisting your commands to suit their own purposes. Shades from our time use their own blood to gain control of themselves. They command themselves to win a battle or remain poised during their grief. The royal family often use it to command themselves to bear heirs." She lifted the goblets from the table and handed one to me.

"Murder! Murder!"

More feet scurried outside. More voices rose as the castle began to wake up with the shock and excitement of Alf's death but I hardly heard it. I remembered the story Dana and Elise had told me about my mother. How she had seen three drops of her blood on the windowsill and said that she would bear a child with lips as red as blood, hair as black as ebony, and skin as white as snow. Had that been shade magic?

She had died giving birth to me. If it had been magic it had cost her her life.

"It can still go wrong." I said. "Even when the command is to yourself."

Ava nodded. "A blood binding is always a great risk. Casting one takes great skill but sometimes it is necessary." She pulled a needle from inside the cuff of her sleeve. "Now is one of those times. May I see your hand again, Cousin? We will make a vow to tell no one what we have seen tonight."

"You can trust me without my blood." I said.

Ava smiled warmly. "Of course. But can you trust me?"

I hesitated.

Ava laughed .Like crystal. Like firelight. "We are family, Snow. Cousins. I would not harm you, but it is not a matter of trust. It is a matter of skill. Things slip from our mouths unbidden, regardless of our intentions. Little things that could give you away without you realizing. This will make sure nothing comes out. This will keep you safe. You and Mirah." She slid the needle into her own finger and squeezed three drops of blood, first into her own goblet, then into mine. The thick beads of red plopped into the thinner red of the wine, mingling slowly into a murky fog. She held out her hand again for mine.

Shade magic. It sounded dangerous. This whole castle was dangerous, stuffed full of murderers and men like Alf. I couldn't count on Otto to protect me. Not if his court was against me. I remembered the stern matronly lady from dinner as she had asked about Hans. Her suspicious glance as she had turned to the lady beside her. "Killer" she had whispered.

"For Mirah's sake if not your own." Ava said.

I gave her my hand. The prick did not hurt. I barely felt it as the steel sliced through my flesh. My blood mixed with Ava's inside the goblets. She dabbed the remaining blood on my finger away with a handkerchief and we drank. I couldn't taste the blood. Only the wine, dark and rich as it went down my throat.

"I vow," Ava said, "to tell no one what has happened tonight."

I repeated the vow and we both drank again, draining the goblets until they were empty. A thrill of excitement surged through me, rich and powerful as I felt the magic bind me. It prickled up and down my skin like a swarm of tiny insects and then it was gone. I must have taken a step back. When we drank Ava had been standing close enough to cross her arms with mine but when I reoriented myself I was standing a full arm's length from her.

She smiled. "There. Now we are blood sisters. I will go and be shocked with the rest of the court. Wait a few moments then find your Rose. The noise must have woken her by now. She will be worried about you." She slipped out the door and I waited, listening to the cackle of the fire and the muffled shouts and footsteps of the courtiers in the corridor.

Murder in secret in the cold halls of a castle.

The same way Lucille had killed Papa.

It was almost as if I had never escaped her grasp at all. As if my whole life would be made of dark deeds hidden from the light of day.

Was it my imagination or was that a wolf howling in the distance?

ROSE

"Murder! Murder!"

I woke to the sounds of shouts echoing through the corridors. It was still dark. I rolled over groggily to speak to Snow beside me but she wasn't there.

I sat up. "Snow." My heart thumped in my chest. Was that a murder they were screaming about in the corridors?

The door creaked open. I turned.

"Snow." I placed my hand on my chest in relief.

She stepped into the room. Her face was paler than usual. Shaken. Her jaw was tense. The irritation I had felt towards her when I'd gone to sleep softened.

"What's happening?"

Snow hesitated. Her brows scrunched in confusion. For a long time she did not speak. The silence between us echoed like a dark empty cavern.

"Go and see for yourself." She said at last.

I blinked. She'd never been so short with me before. I stared at her, waiting for more. She knew more. I could see it in her eyes. She stared back at me, her dark eyes as harsh and immovable as stones.

My anger returned to me in a rush. Was she really so angry with me for wanting to live in a castle that she would stop speaking to me? She had never behaved so childish before.

I lifted my chin in defiance and rolled the blankets off. I threw on my dressing robe and stalked past her through the closet, through the antechamber, and finally out into the corridor. My feet stomped against the stone floor as I walked. I brushed past one of the ladies from diner. Grace she has been called.

She stepped in time with me, placing her hand on her heat. "There's been a murder." She said. "That forester fellow from last night. They're saying Asher did it."

Alf. I flinched at the name. Dead. Like Boris.

A moment later we were in the thick of the crowd. Grace had to push her way through the throng of courtier's but it only took a light tap and the recognition in their eyes before they stepped aside to make way for me. I headed straight for Otto. He stood over Alf's body. Asher stood across from him with a guard on either side. They held him still with his arms behind his back.

"I'll ask you again." Otto said. His voice was clear and authoritative but standing this close to him I could see creases of uncertainty on his brow. "Was he dead when you found him?"

Asher remained silent. He stared at Otto with his quiet, dark eyes. His expression was as dead as stone. His long nightcap trailed over his shoulder, reaching almost as far as his beard.

Otto straightened. "Tell me what happened. Did he attack you first?" His tone was patient but firm, reminding everyone present that he was king even when he wore nothing but a night robe.

Asher was silent for another moment. A susurration of whispers erupted around us, filling the space like a song. "He threatened my Mirah." Asher said at last, so sudden that it was almost a bark. "He deserved to die."

The whispers turned to hisses.

"Murderer!"

"Hang him!"

"Guilty!"

Otto raised his hand for silence. He nodded to the guards. They took a tighter hold of Asher and led him down the corridor. Another pair of guards stepped forward to take Alf's body away. It had already begun to stiffen. The spine hung awkwardly as they lifted it off the carpeted stone and maneuvered it around the corner.

The courtiers watched until the body was completely out of sight. They drifted away, slowly, whispering excitedly to each other. Bastian winked at me as he passed.

I turned toward Otto. I was shaking. Why was I shaking? "The forester did threaten Mirah." I didn't say that he had also threatened me. I tried to push the memory away. It wasn't important.

"Justice is the responsibility of the court." Otto said. "Asher will be tried once the wedding is over." He shook his head. A sigh pushed through his lungs like water released from a dam. "Why couldn't he have waited until morning? I wrote a warrant to have Alf questioned about the incident with Mirah."

I glanced at Mirah's door only a few paces away. "Morning might have been too late."

Otto pressed his forehead into his palms.

"Can't you grant clemency?" I asked. "You are the king."

Otto shook his head. "I gave Lucille's men the chance to start fresh in my service. Many of them had no choice but to serve her but even for those who did choose -it's less dangerous to have them near so I can see if they begin to wreak havoc. Alf was a harsh man and often mean spirited. His threats to Mirah were unacceptable but I cannot allow his murder to go unpunished. It will frighten every other man who used to serve Lucille into rebelling. His murder must be treated the same as any other subject's."

"But surely his actions make him a criminal. You said yourself you had written a warrant for him."

Otto looked at me helplessly. He shook his head. "Justice cannot be done with a knife in the dark. Asher has committed a crime. No matter how understandable he must be tried after the wedding." He sighed. "A murder and an execution is a terrible way to start a marriage."

An execution. So he had decided Asher's fate already.

I trudged my way back to our chambers with heavy feet and a heavier heart. How could Otto allow Mirah to lose a father because he was protecting her? Snow had never been tried for killing Boris or Lucille. This was no different. The man had been a monster.

I was glad he was dead, I realized. Very glad.

I was still shaking.

I slipped through the antechamber and into the closet. Snow was arguing with Louisa about being dressed.

"I don't want to be painted like a doll." Snow said. "Let the gown and slippers be enough." .

"You are royalty." Louisa insisted. "The court expects adornment. You cannot disappoint them."

"Damn them and their expectations." I'd never hear Snow speak with such rancor about people who didn't deserve it.

"Alf has been murdered." I said. "Asher has been arrested."

Louisa gasped. She dropped the dried violets she had been trying to weave into Snow's hair.

Snow said nothing.

I stared at her. *Alf.* I wanted to say. *The man who threatened me*. Only I had not told her that he had threatened me. I had wanted to shoulder that burden myself. It had reminded me too much of things I wanted to forget. *I need you.* I wanted to say. *I need you to hold me because I am shaking all over. I am trying to forget things that refuse to be forgotten.*

I said nothing.

Snow said nothing.

Louisa dressed me. She pinned extra died feathers into my hair to make up for the flowers Snow had scorned. She pursed her lips and clicked her tongue as she arranged them carefully, leaving most of my curls down around face.

It was odd that Snow didn't want the flowers. She usually loved beautiful things. I brought her flowers from my garden all the time.

When Louisa had finished she clasped a gold necklace linked with five rings around my neck. I glanced at Snow. She hadn't even consented to wear her mother's silver. I left her to sulk in our chambers and went for a walk.

The morning light was still young and fresh as I made my way across the castle ward. I closed my eyes, letting the wind toy with my hair like a child plays with string. It was a cold morning. The ward was busy at first, bustling with the usual throng of castle servant but the further I went from the keep the quieter it became. I closed my eyes and listened to the wind.

I stopped, opening my eyes with a gasp. There it was. The same call I had heard the day before. The whisper of magic.

I remembered the last time I had felt the full force of that music thrumming through my blood. I remembered the eyes of First-Light's mother as I had guided a knife into her heart to save my own life. I remembered the force with which I had instructed a hawk to rip it out and bring it to me and Greta.

How had that been any different than Boris when he had forced himself into my poisoned body for his own pleasure? How was I any different?

I clutched my arms around my shoulders to stop from shaking. Hadn't I come out here to escape these memories? I wanted to pull away from them. To shut them out along with every last scrap of magic. The call thrummed loudly inside the wind. I didn't have to listen to it. I could shut it out. I could remain closed off from that piece of myself forever.

But something had woken in me yesterday. A hunger. I had tasted the freedom of embracing my own power.

I let the memories sit in my mind, terrible and immobilizing. My body continued to shake. I counted my heartbeats. Five. Eight. Twenty. They quickened with each thump. I let the memories settle into my body, allowing them to be a part of myself. Allowing the magic. I realized I was holding my breath and softened my lungs, pulling air in and out in a slow, controlled rhythm. My heartbeat slowed with the rise and fall of the air inside me.

Yes. I had used my power to save myself. Yes. I had harmed the forest that I had meant to protect.

A crack opened in my core like a loosening fist. I breathed deep, caressing my center gently like a whisper, and opened myself to the wind.

My being soared with the wind as it swept across the ward. It swept through the smok- filled air over the kitchen stoves. It swept through the dusty, unruly feathers of geese. It swept over the castle walls and out into the meadows as it danced with a furious flurry.

And then I felt it. A strange prickling. Heavy. Startling. A presence like rich warm breath running through my being.

Another being flying with the wind, tangled inside its magic.

The crack in my core closed back up again. Quickly, as if a door were slamming shut. I tried to coax it back open but it held fast, refusing to budge.

A moment later a girl stepped around the corner. She moved toward me with a hurried awkwardness that was almost elegant. Her small pointed nose and chin had an almost bird like quality beneath the circlet of long gold hair bound in a braid around her head. She was followed by a squawking flock of geese.

The boy Conrad trailed behind her, prodding at the geese with his staff. A large goose bit her beak into the long wooden pole, biting down until it splintered. "Florinda!" He cried. "That's a new staff!"

The girl stopped when she reached me. "That was you." She said. "In the wind."

"It was." I said. I had never met anyone else with magic besides Gran and Lucille. A strange impulse stirred inside me to reach out with my magic and caress hers but the crack had sealed shut. The magic had only stayed long enough for me to brush across it.

The girl tilted her head quizzically. "It's gone." She said. "You sealed it off. Why?"

I shook my head. "I didn't do that. It just left."

The wind stirred around me, tangling itself into my long, velvet skirt. My rampant curls swept over my face and got caught in my mouth. Out of the corner of my eye I could see Conrad drop his staff, abandoning his struggle with the unruly goose to clamp his hands over his hat.

The wind stopped. "It's still there." The girl said. "But you won't let it out. Why?"

I peeled my curls away from my face, tucking them behind my ears with the died feathers Louisa had woven into them. "I'm afraid." I said, as surprised by my own answer as I was by my willingness to give it. I had spoken to no one about this. Not even Snow.

Not even myself.

"Afraid of what?"

"The fire."

The girl nodded. "Mine is not a fire. It is a storm. A great and terrifying storm."

Conrad tentatively lifted his hands off his head. He let them hover over his hat for a moment, ready to clamp back down if the wind returned. "Stop making the wind, Gerti." He said crossly. "My mother gave me this hat. My dead mother."

The girl, Gerti, sighed an exasperated sigh. "You told me she beat you. That's why you came to work for the king."

"She was still my only mother and this is still my only hat."

Gerti sighed again. There was a sadness to the sound this time. A wistfulness. "Let's get to the pasture. The geese are hungry." She started walking again. The geese followed after her. Conrad picked up his staff and trailed after them.

"Wait." I strode to catch up with them. "Your magic. Who taught you?"

"My mother." Gerti said without turning to look at me. "Who taught you?"

"My gran. Only . . . I didn't know she was teaching me. She sang to me and told me stories and sort of planted the magic inside me. I didn't know it was there until suddenly I was using it."

Gerti stopped. We had reached the same gate Otto and I had slipped out of the day before. She turned toward me. Her big brown eyes were wide with astonishment. "Song magic. She taught you song magic. It's the rarest form because it is the most difficult to teach."

I wasn't surprised. Gran had been powerful in many ways. Not just her laughter.

"It's gone now." I said, surprised by the deep feeling of loss I felt.

Gerti shook her head. "If she planted the magic in you it's still there." She opened the gate. I followed her through it. The geese waddled after us trailed by Conrad, still clutching his hat. He muttered to himself as he closed the gate behind him.

It was peaceful out here on the meadow compared to the busy bustle of the castle. The sky was gray and crisp as it stretched over us like a story waiting to be told. "Magic never goes away." Gerti said. "It can rot or grow rampant and out of control but once it takes root in a person it never leaves."

"How do I find it again?" I asked. The taste of my fire still lingered in my core.

Gerti looked at me. Her brow creased as if I had asked her to tell me my own name. "Do you want to find it?" She asked.

"Yes."

A familiar stench struck my nostrils as we neared the stone archway. I made a face, eyeing the horse head where it rested on the pike. Some rituals were barbaric no matter where they originated.

"If your mother only knew, her heart would break in two."

I stopped. The voice was eerie. Shrill like a horse's snicker. Human language felt unnatural shrouded in it and it took me a moment to make sense of the words.

The geese squawked excitedly, lifting their feathers and waddling in circles. Conrad patted the feisty one's head. "Don't be frightened Yolinda. It's just a dead horse. A dead horse that talks." He shuddered, casting a dark glance at Gerti, and pulled a handful of grain from his pocket. He squatted near the ground and let the goose eat from his hand. The others crowded around him, sticking their long necks out to reach his offering.

I stared in horror. The horse's maggot filled eye sockets stared back at me from the top of the spike.

Gerti approached the head. She touched it's muzzle fondly as if it were attached to a living horse. "Falada, my friend. Fair winds be with you."

The rotting horse head snickered. A faint, pain filled snicker as if it could still feel its flesh as it rotted away from its bones.

Gerti turned toward me. She touched the remains of its coat, hanging slack against its skull. "Mama gave him to me when I first learned to ride." She said. "He has been my friend since I was a child. My storm did this to him. My magic."

Conrad shuddered. "He's creepy. Why don't you bury him already?"

Gerti turned to him angrily. "And leave him in the ground where he has nothing to comfort him but darkness? At least up here he can see the light and hear the voice of someone who loves him." She stroked his ears gently, hardly even touching his fragile skin, and turned back toward me. "What happened with yours?" She asked. "Your fire. Who did it hurt?"

"The forest that gave it to me." I answered. But it had been more than that. It was the realization of what I could do with it. Who I could hurt. Exactly how much power I had.

Gerti stared at me, unblinking, with her wide strange eyes. "It hurts to betray what we love but do not hide from the gift you could be offering the world. Withholding your strengths can also be a betrayal." She pulled herself away from Falada. "You have the freedom to act but are choosing not to. There are those who do not have that choice."

I turned to face Falada, brushing flies away with the back of my hand. Taking a step closer I could see the morning frost crystalizing on the tip of the carcass's muzzle. I flicked it away, gently so as not to damage the fragile remains of flesh. "What keeps you here?" I asked. "Why won't you finish dying?"

He snickered but didn't answer. Not in the unnatural human language he had spoken in before. A temptation crept inside me to sing to him. To speak to him with my magic the way I had used to speak to my forest.

A witch isn't something you can stop being. Trouble's voice echoed in my mind with a haunting clarity.

"How did you do it?" I asked. "How did you bring him back?" It was a terrible fate for any creature, to live a living death as one's flesh rotted away. Life and death were not play things. I didn't need a magical teacher to know that.

Gerti didn't answer. Tears welled in her eyes and she moved along the path toward the pastures. Conrad and the geese followed after her. I trailed after them. We were a strange parade. Girl, geese, Conrad, princess waddling across the fields in progression. Gerti hummed a strange eerie melody as we walked, sad yet lively. Full of long tones and big jumps. It sounded like the dance of the dead.

"What is that song?" I asked her. "I've never heard anything like it before."

"Nothing." She said. "Just a song from home."

"Where is that?" I asked.

She didn't answer.

"You don't like answering questions do you?"

She smiled slyly. "What makes you say that?"

We reached the pastures and the geese began to graze. Gerti and Conrad sat in the grass to watch them. We hadn't been there long when the wind picked up again. It swept through the grass, circling through the geese's feathers and sending a chill into my bones. Conrad was lounging on the grass with his eyes half closed. They popped open. He lifted his hand up over his head but the motion was too late. His hat had already risen off his head. It flew out across the meadow toward the woods.

"Curse you, fowl witch" He jumped to his feet and chased after it. "I spoke to the king about this. He's going to have you beheaded. He said -"

His voice trailed off, lost in the harsh howl of the wind as he chased after his hat. It would land on the grass just long enough for him to reach it then lift up again as another gust of wind struck.

I turned toward Gerti. She stood watching with a sad almost pained expression.

"Why do you do that?" I asked.

Gerti didn't move. "It's a message." She said.

I knew better than to ask who the message was for or what it meant. I watched Conrad run across the meadow, first one way then the other with grim determination not to lose his only hat for good.

Gerti sat back down on the grass. She crossed her legs and placed her hands in her lap. "Come. We will go into trance while he is gone."

I wrinkled my forehead. "Trance?"

"You've been doing magic without trance?" Gerti narrowed her eyes. "You aren't a shade are you?"

The crease in my brow deepened. I had never known there were so many rules to magic or so many different kinds. "What's that?"

"A slave to your own power. Do you use blood in your spells?."

I shook my head. I'd never really used a spell. Not with ingredients and instructions anyways. Just Gran's song and occasionally a little rhyme to help it along.

"You must learn to go into trance." Gerti said. "It will help you find your magic -and tame it."

I sat with Gerti in the grass and placed my hands on my thighs as she did, palms up.

"Trance is like pruning a garden." Gerti said "It keeps the weeds from taking over and smothering your magic. It keeps it from getting stagnant and rancid. Close your eyes and sit still. Find the magic and allow it to sit still inside you. Don't use it. Don't speak to it. You don't even have to listen to it. Just find it."

I closed my eyes. Wind brushed against my face. I wrinkled my nose and squeezed my eyes to keep them closed. I reached inside for my song but nothing was there. My finger twitched. "How long does it take?" I asked.

"Forever. Some days you never touch your magic. Others it fills your whole soul. But every day you sit and look for it."

I released an exasperated lung-full of air. "That sounds tedious."

"Yes." Gerti sat still. Her eyes weren't closed but they were glazed over. She was in another world. Her body was still. Serene. I could feel the soft whistle of her magic drift through the meadow around her, calm and soothing, so unlike the wildness of my fire.

I closed my eyes again. It felt like torture, trying to sit still. I wanted to get up and run or dance or . . . do anything. Be anywhere but here. My jaw clenched as I willed myself to look inward.

A flame. Crackling. Jumping. Small but unruly. It licked the insides of my soul. A burn. Blistering pain. First-Light's mother, warm with blood. Her heart in my hand, still beating as I handed it to Greta.

I opened my eyes with a gasp.

Gerti was gazing at me. "I felt that." She said. "What happened?"

"I couldn't sit still."

"What happened?" She asked again. "When your magic stopped. What happened then?"

She meant in Lucille's manor. Not just now. "Does it matter?" I snapped.

"Yes." Her tone softened. "If you want to find it again you need to know why it left."

My body shook. I pulled my knees up to touch my chest, huddling like a child to keep still. I looked away from her, staring out at the meadow. It was still and quiet. The geese waddled over the grass looking for insects.

Gerti waited. The wind of her magic whistled around me. It was gentle. Soothing.

"I called a deer to me." I said at last. "A doe with a fawn. Then I killed it. I forced a hawk to rip its heart out and bring it to me. I commanded the forest to turn against itself and it did."

"The forest fights against itself on its own accord. That is the way of the wild."

I shook my head. "The forest gave me my song -my fire -and I turned against it. It was nothing but a friend to me and I took what I needed from it just like . ." I stopped.

"Just like what?"

I clasped my shins, pulling them closer to myself. I rested my chin against my knees. "The forest gave me my magic." I whispered.

"Your gran gave you your magic."

Gerti did not ask me to go back into trance. She closed her eyes and went back under herself while I stared at the grass next to my feet. Conrad came back with his hat. He sat a few feet away from us and nibbled some bread he had brought in his satchel. Gerti surfaced a few minutes later. She had a calm, serene smile on her face as if all were right with the world. I wished her and Conrad a good afternoon and left them there on the meadow. Wind whisked past my ears, cold and hollow, as I strode back toward the castle. I felt one last prickle of Gerti's magic and then it was gone. I felt surprisingly empty without it. Alone. Sad.

Otto was at the gate when I reached it. He was dressed in plain wool and had a bow and quiver strung over his shoulder. He jumped when he saw me then swore.

"Where are you sneaking off to?" I asked him. He seemed tense. Worried. Because of the murder. Because of his pending marriage hovering over him like a storm.

Otto looked at me gravely. His eyes flashed like a king's. He lacked the giddy boyishness he had had yesterday. There was no mischief in his eyes. Only sadness. "There's a bear in this forest who doesn't know how to hunt." He said. "I must find him something to eat."

I squished my brows together, puzzled. "The dancing bear from last night?"

Otto nodded. "I used to love watching the bear dances when I was a boy. I had no idea what cruelties were inflicted upon the poor creatures until I was one of them."

"Did you dance?" I asked "When you were a bear?"

Otto shook his head in confusion. "The memories are muddled. Not really memories at all. Just feelings. But . . . I know things about how the bears are treated that I never knew before I was a bear myself. Last night, when the dance master walked in with his big hooked pole all I felt was fear. My feet hurt. They felt hot like they were on fire. It was all I could do not to dance along with the animal."

"I'm sorry." I said. "Fire burns."

SNOW

A puppet troupe performed in the ward to celebrate the completion of Otto's bear statue. Gold silk curtains parted over the window of an ornately carved cart to reveal a prince on strings as he was cursed by the evil witch Lucille. Smoke clouded in the window. When it cleared a bear on strings stood in the prince's place. He followed the witch Lucille as she terrorized his subjects with her army until, finally, he surprised her at dinner and mauled her to death. The smoke returned and so did the prince on strings. The curtains closed with him sitting at the witch's table eating her heart. The courtiers cheered with excitement. They applauded like a stampede of cavalry.

It was a heavily abridged version of events with no mention of me or Rose. Had Otto written it? Neither he nor Rose were anywhere to be seen in the menagerie of statues as the puppet troupe rolled away their cart and pages brought out trays of pastries and goblets of wine. Nimble and the other musicians began a lively melody.

"It doesn't look a thing like him." The stern woman from dinner said, looking the bear statue up and down. The sculptor had made it much bigger than our red bear had been with sharper teeth and longer claws but it had the same warm human eyes. Otto's eyes.

"Well he's not a bear anymore, Grace." Bastian said, coming up beside her. "Have you seen Mirah? Asher asked me to check in on her."

"She's in her chambers, poor child." The woman -Grace- said.

Bastian shook his head. "Asher a killer." I wouldn't have thought the old bastard had it in him."

My body tingled, prickling with the same sensation I had felt when I had made the blood vow.

"I don't think he did it at all." Grace said. "He's one of us after all." She cast me a suspicious glance.

My head pounded. I felt dizzy. My thoughts scattered. That tingling, prickling sensation. Shade magic, flowing through my blood. Had I been about to say something that would give myself away?

"The brute deserved it." Bastian said lazily. "Otto won't try him. He was only one of Lucille's men after all."

My limbs tingled. I clutched my head, trying to keep my balance. "Excuse me." I muttered and stepped away.

I stepped past the fox statue of Rose's mother. Two young ladies lounged next to it sipping wine.

"It's terrible! Absolutely terrible! I thought we were done with all the bloodshed!"

"It was Mirah who did it. Asher is only protecting her."

Dizziness. Nausea. A headache as if my mind wanted to break into pieces. I strode past the lion representing Rose's father.

"A violent man always dies a violent death." A lord said. "Asher will be next."

My head spun. I felt the vow running through me. Buzzing. Prickling. Swirling. As if it were afraid I would betray information about what I had seen with a mere glance. Trying to speak was useless. I felt as if I'd swallowed a whole barrel of wine. The world spun around me. Statues wavered in every direction as I tried not to listen to the snatches of conversation.

At last I found a dragon statue out of earshot of the courtiers. I sat on the ground behind it, clutching my head in my hands.

"You look like you're going to be sick."

I looked up. Trouble stood in front of me with a tray full of pastries. My head pounded. I could barely focus on the hobgoblin as he stared up at me. He wore his usual scowl but I could see a touch of genuine concern hidden behind it.

Lad came up beside his brother. He balanced two empty trays almost as big as himself. "Hello Snow." He said. "Have you tried the cherry pastries yet?"

Trouble dropped his full tray on top of one of Lad's empty ones. Lad teetered beneath the sudden weight, bending his knee to catch his balance.

"Finish passing those out." Trouble said. "And tell Nimble to play something else. This tune is too cheerful. It's making me nervous. Come with me, milksop." He motioned to me.

I pulled myself onto my feet and followed. My feet swayed as I walked, still dizzy from the buzzing of the vow in my blood. I looked back to see Lad shouldering all three trays as he wove his way through the statues in the direction of the musicians.

The kitchen was a short walk from the menagerie of statues. It was warm inside. It smelled of yeast and raw meat and vegetables and sweat. Sprinklings of flour covered the tables like a light dusting of snow.

It felt almost like home.

Trouble led me to a chair and commanded me to sit. I obeyed. I was already feeling much better now that we were away from talk about the murder. My head felt clear again. I no longer felt as if I might vomit.

"Sludge." Trouble said. "Get Snow some tea before she dies."

Sludge looked up from the pot he was stirring. He set down his spoon and reached for a kettle. A moment later I had a warm cup of apple tea in my hands. I cradled it, letting the steam steep up into my nostrils.

Trouble sat down across from me and lit his pipe. He puffed it slowly then pulled it out of his mouth, watching the smoke rise with a contemplative expression. "The courtiers are all idiots." He said.

"Now, now." Sludge picked up his wooden spoon and stuck it back in his pot, stirring slowly. "Let's not speak poorly of our king. Treason and all that."

Trouble shrugged. "He's alright as far as kings go, but the rest of them? All chatter and no brains. You should have seen the nonsense they were passing off as a puppet show. Otto maul Lucille? Ha! She was dead hours before he arrived."

"It's only a bit of entertainment. Folk like to see their king as a hero." Sludge tasted the stew he was stirring. His face twisted in disapproval. "Needs more salt. And fennel."

I leapt to my feet and stepped toward the spice rack.

"Careful." Trouble took another puff of his pipe. "Don't let her touch anything you're sending to the keep. Your reputation will be destroyed."

"I'm not always a bad cook." I protested. My hands closed around the tiny white crystals and long green flakes he needed.

"Sometimes is often enough to make you dangerous."

Sludge took the salt and fennel out of my hand. He stirred them into his stew and slid the wooden spoon towards me. I lifted it to my lips. The stew was rich and creamy. The perfect blend of onion, fennel, and pike. I licked my lips in appreciation. "It's delightful."

Sludge sighed. "If only I had enough bread to serve it with. I lost another three sacks of flour yesterday. They won't have anything to soak it up with tonight."

"Someone's stealing flour?" I asked.

"And milk. And onions. And salted pork. They made off with a sack of apples last week." Trouble glowered. "We're being slowly fleeced from the inside while those idiot nobles throw feasts and watch terrible puppet shows."

"It's a wedding." I said. "They're supposed to celebrate." Still, it was strange that Otto had not mentioned the disappearing food. Was he trying to keep it a secret? "Most of them probably don't know that anything has been stolen."

"Ha!" Trouble said. "Idiots."

"If I find the scoundrels responsible I'll tear them limb from limb." Sludge said. "Every time I plan a dish something new goes missing and I have to redesign everything It's a disgrace is what it is."

"We were close to finding out who it was." Trouble grumbled. "Then that oaf Alf had to get himself killed."

My head buzzed. I dropped the spoon in my hand. It clattered onto the floor, dribbling warm stew all over the stone surface.

"Careful." Sludge bent to pick it up.

"Glen and I saw him loading something into a cart but the cart disappeared before we could search it." Trouble continued. I'll bet my beard he was working for the fellow responsible for the thefts and that's why he was killed."

My blood swirled. I stepped back to keep my balance. I had almost forgotten that cook, musician and footman were only a ruse for the hobgoblins' real titles at Otto's court.

Spies.

I tried to listen despite the dizzy tingling buzzing through my body. The room spun.

"I can't think of a soul who will miss that oaf." Sludge said. "A rotten brute. Always sticking his hands in my pies. He wanted to use my ovens to train bears. As if my kitchen were some kind of summer fair."

I clutched my head and stepped backward toward the door. The nausea was too much. I needed to go somewhere I could think. A hundred tiny pin pricks worked their way up and down my limbs.

"What's wrong?" Sludge asked.

"I just need some air." I managed to stutter through the haze of dizziness. "Thank you for the tea." I turned and tried not to run out the door. I spilled out into the cold and strode across the ward. The prickling stopped as soon as I was out of earshot of the kitchen. I breathed deep, letting my head and stomach settle back into place. I kept walking, not thinking about where I was going until I stood in front of the cathedral.

The heavy oak doors groaned as I pushed them open. It was dark inside. Empty and unlit since morning services had ended. I felt along the walls, looking for the crack that led to the library. I was about to give up when my fingers finally slid into the gap in the stone. I crammed them in a little deeper and pulled.

The door creaked open.

I climbed up the long winding staircase and stepped into the small enclosed space.

The book of love poems I had been reading the day before lay on the bench but I wasn't in the mood for amorous phrases today. I turned toward the shelves to find something else.

My fingers hovered over the binding of the book on divination. The dark leather was soft. Worn from use. What would it mean to know my future? I would not stay in this castle forever. I longed for our little cottage in the woods. The cozy little space that was ours and ours alone. Rose would see reason by the time the wedding was over and we would return home.

I did not need to read my future to know that.

I did not.

I pulled my hand away.

I chose another book at random and opened it. Inside was a thin, elegant scrawl that swirled in ridiculous flourishes on every letter.

Apples -50

Dried figs -142

Cinnamon -6 vials

A ledger book. How odd that it was kept in the library and not the steward's study. Perhaps it was old. From one of Otto's ancestors.

The door clicked. I looked up, startled. Ava spilled into the library. Her eyes widened when she saw me. She collapsed onto the bench, clutching her head. "Thank God it's just you. The blood vow is so much stronger than I thought it would be. I can barely have a conversation with anyone without feeling it."

Here was one person at least who would not talk about the murder. I shuddered. "Why are they so preoccupied with death?"

Ava shrugged. "A castle is a place of power. Power breeds death."

I collapsed onto the bench beside her. I hadn't realized until that moment that I was shaking.

"Oh you poor thing!" She touched my arm, steadying me. "The vow has made you weak all over. It was a stupid idea. Absolutely foolish of me. It's bad enough for me but I'm used to shade magic. I'm so sorry, Cousin. I should have trusted you not to give anything away. Please say you'll forgive me?" She took my hands in hers, squeezing them tight. Her eyes were wide. Her brow scrunched with worry.

I smiled weakly. "I suppose it's not much worse than trying to converse with the courtiers on a normal day."

Ava laughed. Relief flooded her features. "Come now. They aren't as bad as all that." She glanced at the book in my hand. "That's dry reading isn't it? Are you thinking of becoming a steward?"

I shook my head.

Her lips quirked. "It always sounds like a good idea doesn't it? Going somewhere new. Living a different life. And yet somehow the same troubles you had in one place seem to follow you. You can change the cage you're in but you can never really get free."

I looked at her curiously. "What cage were you in in the south?"

A shadow passed over her face. She closed her eyes. "I was invisible there. Lonely. The court only saw my title, never me. I was not loved for who I was, only what I was. It was foolish for me to think coming here would change that."

"Otto will be kind to you." I assured her.

"Yes." She said. "But he will never love me. Kindness is a paltry balm to loneliness. It may sooth it for a moment but it cannot cure it. Kindness can be as hollow as cruelty when there is no love behind it."

I squeezed her hands, still holding mine. I had no words to comfort her with. She and Otto would both be trapped in this marriage. Caged like birds or dancing bears. Why did Rose want to be royalty? The price of all the jewels and velvet was becoming a slave to tradition.

She smiled sadly. "You, at least are not like the other courtiers. You see me when I speak, not Otto's crown. I am not so lonely when I am with you."

"Good." I smiled weakly. "You may see more of me than you expected if I stay here like Rose wants."

"You don't want to stay?"

I shook my head.

"Well then. We'll have to change Rose's mind, won't we? We still have another week before the wedding. Anything could happen."

I nodded. Of course. Rose would see reason. I would not have to stay here.

Still, I felt queasy all over and it was not the blood vow. What part of our life in the woods did Rose want to escape by moving here? Was she lonely even with me to keep her company?

And then I realized. She hadn't had any nightmares since we'd arrived at Otto's castle. It was our home that haunted her sleep.

"Come." Ava let go of my hands. "Let's find something more exciting than an old ledger book to whittle away the hours while we wait for the court to find something new to gossip about."

I set the ledger book on the bench next to the love poems and followed her to the shelves. I opened one of the chained books. A book of spells. A spell marked "Sleeping Draught" listed dreamshade mixed with mugwort and a drop of the sleeper's blood.

For Endless sleep.

Endless Sleep? Could that cure Rose's nightmares so that she wouldn't have any when we went home?

Ava peered over my shoulder. "That spell is death in all but name." She said. "A sleep you never wake up from. They say it is so deep that you can even meet the dead in your dreams."

"How would they know that if no one has woken up?" I asked.

Her lips quirked. "It's probably just a story but the spell is irreversible." She pointed to where it indicated a drop of the sleeper's blood. "The ones that use blood always are."

"Shade magic." I said.

She nodded.

I closed the book and set it back on the shelf.

"I know." Ava exclaimed suddenly. She clasped her hands together in excitement. "Have you ever read a play out loud before? I think I saw the Seven Swans here somewhere. I'll do the lady's part if you'll read the part of my dashing protector." She reached for a volume on the shelf across from me.

"You won't have any lines." I pointed out. "Not until after you weave seven shirts out of nettles."

"I don't mind. The silence will be a small price to pay for someone to protect me. For someone to care enough to stop an execution for me." She spoke glibly, lightly as if it were a practical comment about the weather but I sensed she wasn't talking about the play at all.

"There is when you're a child." I said, thinking of how safe I had always felt with Papa. "Then you grow up and learn to look after yourself."

Ava laughed lightly. "Then I never was a child." She opened the book and handed it to me. "Here. You begin. At the start where you find me alone in the wilderness."

It was dark by the time we'd finished reading through our parts. My throat was hoarse from shouting and the candle we'd lit was near the end of its wick. Ava lay on the ground where she had recited her final soliloquy -her confession of love and devotion after flinging the nettle shirts on her brothers and regaining her voice - from memory. It was beautifully spoken. I gaped at her in amazement, believing every tear, almost forgetting that she had not just escaped being burned as a witch at the hands of the man she loved.

"The banquet will be starting." She picked herself up off the rug she had collapsed on and pulled her gold curls out of her face where they had fallen out of their careful arrangement on top of her head. They looked much better loose and free around her shoulders. She looked more like a young, excited girl and less like a poised queen with court manners. "We will be missed if we're not there."

"Yes. Yes, of course." I shook myself, pulling myself away from the scent of burning nettle in my mind. I placed the book back on the shelf.

We made our way down the staircase and across the cathedral hall in silence. Moonlight poured in through the tall glass windows, falling like ghosts against the marble floor. I shivered as we stepped outside. The first fall of snow had begun. It dusted the ground like sugar on a cake, sweet and sticky.

"I'm going to fetch my knife." I told Ava. Not having it with me felt like I was missing a piece of myself.

"Be careful." Ava warned. "Don't let anyone see you."

Music had already begun in the banquet hall. I could hear it drifting through the stone walls as I reached the spot beneath Mirah's window where Ava had thrown my knife. Snow collected quickly on the stone flagstones. I squinted, searching the thin blanket of white for a hint of silver but my knife was nowhere to be seen. I stooped in the shadows and felt the ground with my hands. The tiny ice particles soaked into my skin, turning my fingers red with cold.

Nothing.

Perhaps I had remembered the place wrong. I tried another window. Then another. I circled the keep, trying window after window. The snowfall piled thicker and thicker onto the ground as the night wore on. My fingers and nose grew numb. My eyes became sore from searching in the faint light of the waxing moon. My stomach rumbled as I realized I hadn't eaten since breakfast.

I returned to the first window I had tried. I was certain it was the right one. There was Rose and I's chambers only a few windows away. A candle glimmered from inside. Rose getting ready for bed. The music had long since stopped inside the banquet hall. The feasting must have ended early tonight. Perhaps the murder had dampened even the courtiers' craving for entertainment.

Feet plodded against the ground. Night guards patrolling. I crouched down, low onto the snow, careful not to make a sound as they passed. I couldn't risk being seen looking for the knife any more than I could risk it being found by anyone else. Their matching black tunics still made me shudder. I waited long after their footsteps had disappeared to make sure they were really gone. My arm cramped beneath my stomach. My cheek grew numb from being smashed against the snow. Ice melted into the bodice of my gown. I held back a shiver.

At last I pulled myself back up to my feet. A wolf howled. The moon illuminated the snow like fallen stars inside the ward. I shivered. My teeth clenched with cold. I couldn't search any more tonight. I turned back toward the entrance to the keep.

The wolf howled again.

A chill ran through me. My feet crunched against the snow.

Another howl.

A were. I was certain of it this time. All the more reason to retrieve my knife.

I reached the menagerie of statues just outside the keep's entrance. The white stone of the animal figures glittered in the moonlight as snow sprinkled down on them from the night sky.

Something moved out of the corner of my eye. A shadow.

I turned.

Footsteps in the snow. Light. Steady.

My heartbeat quickened. The shadow passed by again, scurrying just out of my eyesight. I reached for where my knife should have been at my hip and cursed.

Another howl. The statues of creatures loomed at me throughout the ward.

I stepped forward. My eyes darted from statue to statue, each a shadow of fur and claws in the dark. There was the lion. There was Otto's bear. A fox. A buck. A wolf.

No. I stopped, paralyzed with fear. The wolf moved. He turned and looked at me with his big, yellow eyes. His body shifted as he slowly changed shape and he wasn't a wolf anymore at all. He was a man, naked and menacing with a familiar mop of curly brown hair.

Boris.

He grinned his wolfish grin, lopsided and almost charming. "Hello there, Snowy White. Come to kill me again, have you? Only your hunter isn't here to save you, is he? Tsk tsk. You are a poor student. You didn't even bring your knife."

He stepped toward me.

I ran. My feet pounded against the snow-covered cobblestones as I pushed myself forward, darting behind Otto's bear statue first, then his father's lion. Boris's footsteps pounded behind me, crunching against the snow. His strides were longer than mine but I was smaller and lighter on my feet. I darted from statue to statue, slowly making my way toward the entrance to the keep.

At last I could see the big oak doors, tall like a cavern entrance, in the dark. I moved faster and faster as I neared them.

The last statue was a dragon, representing the first of the kings who had ruled here. I darted away from its cover with my heart pounding in my chest. I shouted to the guards to open the door.

My feet slipped on the ice. I fell. My face smashed into the earth. Blood dripped down my nose as I pulled myself back to my feet. My head throbbed. I spun around, expecting at any moment to feel Boris's cold, naked fingers grabbing at my limbs. I could make out the faint traces of his footprints in the snow, illuminated by the light of the moon.

Nothing. No shadow. No ragged rhythm of his breath.

I tensed, afraid to move. Slowly, with my heart beating like a sledgehammer in my breast, I turned.

Nothing.

No footprint. No shadows.

I turned again.

Nothing. Only the trail of footprints -his and mine -leading up to where I had fallen. A cold wind riffled through my hair, biting my nose and cheeks. I looked down at my snow and dirt covered gown and tried to wipe the blood off my face.

My heart pounded as I made my way across the ward. The guards opened the doors for me and I stepped inside the keep. The heavy oak slammed behind me with a loud echoing jolt.

The banquet hall was abandoned. I made my way through it to reach the stairs. Only a few of the candles were still lit. Bits of sweets and empty goblets the nobles had left lay on the floor and benches. The musicians' instruments lay against the wall, casting long shadows against the flickering light. The room seemed smaller somehow without any people in it, no longer a labyrinth of noise and motion. The drapes looked almost like large tree trunks draped against the long glass windows.

I stepped onto the staircase, making my way up. I needed to tell Rose about Boris. Peaceful sleep or not I would have to wake her. She would want to know that he had come back from the dead. I had never heard of such a thing before. Dead was dead.

Two fingers touched me lightly against the wrist.

My heart rattled like an old chain. I looked up, cursing once again that I didn't have my knife.

Mirah stood on the step in front of me, barefoot. Her eyes were swollen. Her long hair tangled and matted around her neck and shoulders. Her night shift was wrinkled and bunched where she had been grabbing it with her fists like a child. "Save him." She said. "Save Papa. Only you can."

I shook my head, sadly. "Otto may show him mercy." If he had any compassion at all he would.

"No." Her dark brown eyes grew angry. Fierce. She rolled her hands into fists. "Tell them. Tell them who really killed Alf."

I opened my mouth to ask her what she meant but the tingling returned inside my blood. I clutched my head and stepped back. My mind buzzed.

When I opened my eyes again Mirah had her hand on my face. She held my gaze. "You too." She said. Tears glinted in her eyes, illuminated by the glow of moonlight wafting in through the window.

I felt so dizzy. My mind buzzed like a beehive. I clamored around inside it, looking for words I was allowed to say. My whole body tensed up as if it were going to explode. "I don't know who killed Alf." I managed at last. That at least was true.

Mirah pulled her hands away from my face. "No." She shouted, angry again. "No." She clutched the railing on the staircase, staring out the window into the night. Angry, desperate tears pooled out of her swollen eyes. "No. No. No. No. No."

I placed my hand on her shoulder. The poor child hadn't gotten any sleep. She had been accosted, seen a murder, and lost her father all in one night. Memories played in my mind. Being locked in my room by Lucille's servants. Missing Papa. Not wanting to eat or move. I had been so afraid.

Mirah pulled away from me. She turned and pushed me against the railing on the stairs then struck me hard across the face. "Tell them." She screeched. "Save papa. Tell them."

I held my hand up to protect myself from another blow. She was mad with grief and shock and . . . something else.

What did she think I knew?

"Mirah," I said.

She stepped back, releasing me from the stair rail, then swung at me again. Her eyes were wild -feral- as she pounded her fists into me.

I dodged to the side. She was a few years younger than me but the same height. Still, my body was stronger and more agile.

Mirah grabbed hold of me, pushing me toward the rails once again with the mad strength of a rabid dog. I pushed back. We both lost our footing, landing with a heavy thud on the staircase. I tried to untangle myself from her but her nails dug into my arm and shoulder like claws, pulling me down. I screamed, then rolled over, pinning her beneath me. I held her wrists as she stared up at me with eyes like daggers. Her breath was short and ragged as she struggled against my grip.

I released her and pulled away, sitting on the steps next to her. "I'm not going to hurt you, Mirah. Tell me what it is that I need to tell Otto. I will help you if I can"

Mirah sat up halfway. She clutched her head then shook it back and forth like a pendulum. She pulled at the roots of her hair. For a moment I thought she was going to be sick.

"He was smuggling." She said at last. She pulled tighter at her hair, then buried her face back into her hands. Her voice was little more than a whisper. "Check the ledger. The ledger in the library."

I scrunched my brow in confusion. She had seen the ledger in the library? "Who was smuggling?" I asked. "Your father or Alf?" Or someone else. The real killer.

"Snow."

I looked up. Ava stood over us draped in her silver night robe. "You do have a huntress's nose for trouble don't you Cousin?" She said.

I looked back at Mirah but her moment of sobriety had passed. She banged her head against the stairs. Bits of blood began to break through the skin on her forehead. "It's no use." She screamed "Absolutely no use. He's going to die. He's going to die."

"Mirah, child." Ava knelt next to us, "Stop that, please. You'll hurt yourself."

Mirah stopped. She rested her bleeding face in her hands and began to sob. Her shoulders shook as she wailed like a mountain storm.

"Mirah." I reached for her shoulder once again. She shot up before I could touch her, blinking at me with wild eyes. Blood dripped down her forehead, mingling with the tears streaked to her cheeks.

"You will see." She rose to her feet. "You will see that it is no use. You will see everything that is kept secret. Papa is innocent."

She turned toward the stair rails. She leaned back, balancing on the balls of her feet.

I realized too late what she was doing. I leapt to my feet but she had already sprung over the rail and into the air.

I watched as she fell. Her matted hair fluttered. Even three stories in the air I could hear her bones crack as she hit the ground. The back of her head smashed into the window. Glass shattered. Cold winter air burst into the hall. Snowflakes swirled with the shards of glass.

Ava touched my hand. I turned toward her. Her other hand was clasped tight over her mouth as if holding back a scream. She'd said I had a nose for trouble but she was never far behind. "What are you doing here?" I asked. All the other nobles had slept through the ordeal. Even the guards hadn't heard anything.

"I was worried about you. You never came to dinner. Did you find your knife?"

I shook my head. I looked back down at Mirah's body, twisted on the hall floor. The wind whistled through the broken glass. I shivered.

Ava squeezed my hand. "The poor child. The poor, poor child. Who will tell Asher?"

I turned back toward her.

Ava bit her lip. She pulled her robe tighter around her chest. Her girlish curls rustled around her pale, worried face. "We must give her what dignity we can. No one must know of her attack. Her madness." She met my gaze. Imploring. Almost pleading. "This is another night we will tell no one of."

I opened my mouth to ask her about the smuggling. To tell her why I needed to tell Rose about seeing Boris. To protest that we couldn't just leave Mirah here. We had to tell somebody . . . something. No sound came out. A tingling shot through my neck and head. I felt dizzy. And weary. So, so weary. Had Ava meant to enact the spell again? I swayed on my feet, disoriented.

She pulled her hand away from my wrist as if she'd suddenly realized what she'd done. She looked at me with wide, worried eyes. Her face was pale like the ice on the windows. Had she been eating at all today? Neither of us had gotten much sleep.

I nodded, surrendering to the blood spell. We turned and made our way up the stairs, walking together in silence. Our gowns swished against our legs in the darkness. The corridors felt narrow, suffocating, pregnant with secrets.

At last I reached my chambers and slipped inside. Louisa was asleep in the antechamber. I made my way past her into the closet and peeled off my snow soaked gown, replacing it with a fresh, warm night shift. The shadows of the chests and basin and candelabras lining the walls crowded around me. Oppressive. Menacing. I listened for a wolf howl but the only thing I heard was the gentle crackling of a fire inside the bedroom.

Rose lay awake in bed. She sat staring into the flames flickering the fireplace with a blanket pulled tight around her shoulders. Her curls were tangled around her ears. She looked up when she saw me, staring with a distant fiery expression in her eyes. She quirked her lips half heartedly into a smile. "Stop reading so many ghost stories, Snow. You look haunted from your day in the library."

I am haunted. I tried to say. *I just saw Boris outside. I just saw Mirah throw herself off the staircase. I'm the only one who knows who killed Alf but I don't know what I know. My brain is muddled from being dizzy all day and I haven't eaten anything.* But the words did not come. A tingling washed over my body like tiny little insects crawling through my blood. I collapsed onto the bed and pulled the blankets tight around my shoulders.

ROSE

"Threw herself off the staircase, poor child." Louisa tightened a ribbon in my hair. "Couldn't live with the shame of what her father had done. Others are saying that it was she who had really killed Alf and she couldn't bear the guilt of letting her father take the blame."

I frowned. Mirah hadn't seemed like someone who could have killed anyone but neither had Snow until she had been given no other option. Neither had I. "Why not confess? Then at least her father would have been released."

Louisa shrugged. "Perhaps he forbade her to, There are those who obey their elders, though I don't imagine you're one of them." She winked. "Not if you're anything like your mother."

"Of course not." I winked back but I was only half listening.

Asher had killed Alf for nothing. It hadn't saved Mirah. I glanced at Snow. She sat on a bench nibbling an apple pastry in a white velvet gown. She had killed Boris but it hadn't saved me either. I had dreamt about him again last night. I had thought I was free of my nightmares at last here in Otto's castle but they had flooded back into my sleep with vigor. I should never have tried to reawaken my magic.

"They may have to postpone the wedding." Louisa chattered on. "They won't be able to repair the window in time."

"Will we go forward with the hunt?" I asked. Last night no one had much felt like celebrating. The feasts had ended early and we'd all gone to bed in quiet contemplation. That had been for the death of a servant no one had much liked. This was one of us. Another guest. An innocent. Hardly more than a child. Were there always this many deaths inside a castle?

"Otto insists." Louisa said. "He refuses to abandon his guests even in the wake of tragedy. There." She stood back. "Lovely as always. You will be a striking sight on top of a horse in that gown."

"If I can manage to stay on one." I muttered. I glanced at Snow again. She had finished the pastry and stood up. She had once again refused to allow Louisa to touch her hair and plaited it in a long simple braid that trailed down her back. She'd even insisted on her boots instead of the court slippers Louisa had tried to put on her.

"I'll need them for riding." She'd said and hadn't allowed for any negotiation.

"You're quiet this morning." I said. My eyes strayed to the bruise still fading on her cheek.

She didn't answer.

My insides flared with anger. Why did she have keep sulking about me wanting to stay here instead of returning to Gran's cottage? She'd hardly said a word to me since we had argued about it. She was shutting me out, refusing to yield until I did what she wanted. It was foolish, petty behavior when so much death hung over us.

"You don't have to come." I reminded her. I didn't bother to keep the venom out of my voice.

"I like to hunt." Snow said. "And I want to talk to Otto."

Otto? A familiar pang of jealousy swept through me. What did she need to talk to Otto about when she would barely talk to me? Otto who was still so obviously in love with her.

I dismissed Louisa and went to find Gerti. There was still time before the hunt. If I hurried I could reach her before she left for the pastures with Conrad.

Gerti stood in front of the goose pen with Conrad, humming the same strange eerie melody she had been humming out in the pastures. Sad yet lively like the dance of the dead. She looked up when she saw me. Her eyes were misted and dreamy. Had she just come out of trance? No, she was on her feet and her lips were twisted in a mysterious half smile. "You look angry." She said.

"I am angry." I stared back toward the keep but I didn't come her to talk about Snow. I came to talk about what I couldn't talk about with Snow because she was sulking, "I can't find my magic again." I said. "I can't go into trance. My nightmares have come back."

Gerti looked at me quizzically. She tilted her head. Her sleek, bird-like nose twitched. "Is that because you touched your magic or because you pulled away from it?"

I opened my mouth, then closed it again. I hadn't thought of that. I had walked away from the meadow yesterday completely closed off to my magic, wanting nothing to do with it.

Gerti smiled gently. "Try again. It takes awhile sometimes."

"Come on Gerti." Conrad opened the gate to the pen. The geese waddled out, leaving footprints in the snow. "Florinda is hungry."

I turned back toward the keep.

The courtiers met for the hunt in the inner ward near the stables. Not everyone came. Many had decided to stay in their rooms. The small size of the hunting party made the tragedy of Mirah's death seem worse somehow. As if we had lost more than just her.

"Chin up, girl." Bastian winked at me as he pulled himself up into his saddle. "The fates might be against this wedding but diplomatic unions will prevail. Tradition will see us through."

Snow stood outside the stable with a black mare, saddled and ready for the hunt. The darkness of the animal's coat glistening in the sunlight contrasted with the white of last night's snowfall and the velvet on Snow's gown. Ava stood beside her. They spoke together in hushed voices. Intent. Familiar. Like Sisters. There were secrets in their mannerisms. Glances at the rest of us that set themselves apart.

Not like sisters at all. Like lovers.

I felt suddenly very alone. Shut out from the little world they were creating with their conversation. She had barely spoken that many words to me since we had arrived.

Otto came up beside me, whistling a strange eerie melody, sad yet lively. "Are you ready for your first hunt, Princess Rose?" His eyes were dreamy. Distant.

I turned toward him, curious. "You seem . . . different." He had been that way last night during the banquet too. Distracted. Cheerful almost. There was a boyishness to him again unlike the grave, worried king he had been when I'd seen him slinking off to feed the dancing bear. If I hadn't already known he was in love with Snow I would have thought he had met a girl.

Otto shrugged guiltily. "I don't suppose you would believe that I am putting on a brave face for my guests."

I shook my head.

Hooves clattered beside us then stopped. We both turned to see Snow leading her black mare. She wore the same solemn, focused expression she wore when she practiced throwing knives. "Otto." She said.

There was a long silence. We waited. She said nothing. I rankled at her reticence.

"How do you know?" She asked at last.

Otto wrinkled his brow, "Know what?"

That expression again. Careful. Methodical. Almost pained. "That it was Asher."

Otto sighed. He opened his hands in a gesture of helplessness. "He was found over the body with a weapon. Who else could it have been?"

Snow looked sick. Furious. She swayed on her feet. It was a long time before she spoke. "Alf used to work for Lucille. He was a brute. He had any number of enemies. He deserved to die."

"Snow." Otto began but didn't finish. A horn sounded. Those who weren't already on their horses pulled themselves up into their saddles. Otto strode forward to take his stallion from the stableman. Snow pulled herself up onto her mare then pulled me up onto the saddle behind her. I had never been on a horse's back before. I held onto her stomach to keep myself from falling off.

Snow clenched her fists. "I want to go home." She said. It frightened me to see her like this. There was so much hatred in her eyes. So much anger. And . . . something else. Fear? What was she not telling me?

It didn't matter. I had found a home here. I had begun to rekindle my magic, to quiet my nightmares. If she didn't want to understand that she didn't want to understand me.

The hunting horn sounded again. Snow leaned forward on our mare and we jolted into motion. We sped across the ward after Otto and his stallion with the other courtiers gaining momentum around us. Hooves clattered. Icy fractals of snow scattered up from the ground, melting against my face. I held on tight to Snow as we bounced up and down, moving forward as if we were flying.

Wind brushed against my skin, running its fingers through my hair. I closed my eyes, feeling for Gerti's magic. There. Just a whisper, winking at me from inside the wind's dance. My flames flickered in greeting and then it was gone.

I had done it again. Almost as if by accident. I had touched my magic.

I opened my eyes. We had left the inner ward now. The outer gates opened for us and we clattered through them like a cavalry. Even with the small hunting party I felt a sense of glory in galloping together. All of us racing forward toward the same thing as if our life depended on it. We slowed our pace when we reached the woods. Snow breathed deeply in the saddle in front of me, catching her breath.

"Did we lose sight of our prey already?" I asked.

"We haven't found it yet." Snow said. "That was a prelude. A quick run to get everyone in pace."

I sank back in the saddle, disappointed.

"The whole thing is a glorified parade." Snow said. "A real hunt takes stealth not all this pomp and noise."

"You didn't have to come." I reminded her. She didn't have to come to the castle at all if she was going to hate everything in it so much.

"A glorified parade?" Bastian pulled his horse up beside ours, horrified. "It's a tradition. A bonding ritual between the king and his couriers. The prey has nothing to do with it."

"Typical foreigner." Grace sniffed from atop her steed on the other side of us. "Doesn't understand anything."

Otto stopped at the head of the hunting party. The rest of the courtiers followed suit. Otto dismounted his stallion and announced that he was going to scout for our prey. Snow slid out of our saddle and joined him. He hardly glanced at her as he handed her a second hunting horn. I stared at him curiously. Normally he would blush and gaze sheepishly when she stood so close to her. It was a welcome change but . . . odd. They both slipped into the forest in opposite directions.

The black mare stomped her foot. I grabbed the reigns but didn't know what to do with them. I looked at Bastian for help. "What do we do now?"

He grinned, flourishing his hands in a flowery twirl. "We feast, my girl."

"Before the hunt?" I glanced around. The other courtiers were dismounting. They pulled blankets out of their saddles and made themselves comfortable on the ground despite the snow.

Bastian helped me off the mare. I sat with him and Grace beneath an old oak. I was glad for my gloves and cloak as the damp of the ground soaked through the blanket and the icy air turned our noses red. Bastian recounted the tale of how he had once uncovered a human finger bone at a crossroad. A few minutes later eight maids from the castle appeared with pails of warm milk that they passed around to the courtiers along with bread, fruit, and cheese.

"Such rustic fare!" Bastian exclaimed. "I feel quite the crusader."

"I do wish there was a fire." Grace complained.

We ate slowly, letting the steam from the milk warm us. Birds twittered in the cold, winter air. It was odd. When Alf had been killed everyone had spoken of nothing else but no one mentioned Mirah, as if saying her name would bring new death. Instead we spoke of Grace's wedding which took place a full twenty years ago and the cut of Bastian's new coat. Ava joined us and we spoke of winters in the south and how much warmer they were. I told them about our winter bonfires in the wood. Staying up late roasting apples as we thanked the earth for her bounty. I turned, expecting Snow to tell them about the game she caught for the occasion, but she was not there.

A pang of loneliness echoed in my breast. I shook it away. We did not always have to be together. Perhaps we were together too often. The thought saddened me. I was angry with Snow but I still missed her.

I was angry at her because I missed her.

The sky grew gray as storm clouds began to gather.

"It will snow again tonight." Bastian said.

It was well past noon when Otto returned. Was it my imagination or did he have an extra sparkle in his eyes? His arms swung, careless and relaxed at his sides. He was whistling again. That same strange eerie melody, sad yet lively like the dance of the dead. Where had I heard it before?

Bastian stood and saluted his king. "No game?"

Otto shook his head. He lifted his horn to his lips and sounded it. A few moments later Snow appeared. Her eyes were sharp and alert. She crouched slightly, resting on the balls of her feet, ready to spring into action. "What are we chasing?"

"Nothing." Otto said. "We're heading back."

Snow drooped. "I was on a deer's trail. It was getting warm."

Otto took his stallion's halter and stroked the animal's coat. "There will be other hunts." He said lightly. We tidied up the pic-nic fare and mounted our horses. A few moments later we were trotting slowly back toward the keep.

Snow sighed in the saddle in front of me. She stared out into the woods with a haunted expression. I let her slink back into her sulk as we trotted slowly with the others. The cold kiss of winter brushed across my face as the sky darkened overhead and the clouds thickened. The night's storm was near.

Snow slowed the mare's pace so that we fell behind the others. "Sludge said food keeps disappearing from the kitchens." She said suddenly. She spoke slowly. Directly. As if she were choosing her words with great care. "He thinks Alf may have had something to do with it."

I wrinkled my brow, puzzled. "Have the disappearances stopped since his death?"

Snow dropped hold of the reigns. The mare strayed to the side a little before she regained control of them. She didn't answer.

There it was again. Her stubborn silence. My confusion boiled quickly into anger. "Stop sulking." I snapped. "If you want to talk about something talk about it. Don't bring it up and drop it again as if it were a burning apple."

She was silent. The mare's hooves clattered rhythmically against the ground. A bird called from up in the trees. "I . . . " She started but didn't finish. She dropped the reigns again. The mare stopped completely.

"You want me to hate this castle as much as you do." I accused. "You're looking everywhere to find fault with the life here so that I won't want to stay but it's not going to work. I belong here. I've found my magic again here. I don't have as many nightmares. If you don't want to stay you can go back to Gran's cottage by yourself."

Snow tensed. She gripped the reigns so tight her knuckles looked white. "You don't mean that." She said.

But I did.

"It's dangerous here." Her voice echoed in the silence. Soft. Deadly

"Not for me." I said. "Alf and Mirah could have died anywhere."

Snow leaned forward, still gripping the reigns as if they would save her from a fate worse than death. She said nothing. The rest of the party were almost out of view. At last she straightened in the saddle. "If that's what you want." She said at last. "I will leave in the spring when the mountain pass clears."

I blinked. She didn't mean that. She was only saying it to make me change my mind.

Wasn't she?

Snow leaned forward and the mare started moving again. Hooves crunched against the snow. We swayed with the rocking motion of her withers as we trotted to catch up with the others. My chest ached at the thought of losing Snow for good. My whole body felt hollow and broken.

I didn't change my mind.

It was dusk when we returned to the castle. I barely had time to go to our chambers and change into a fresh gown before the feast began. Snow was lying on the bed when I left, arguing with Louisa about needing a fresh gown.

The feasting hall was cold. The court gathered around the shattered window at the end of the hall, examining the ragged teeth-like edges as the storm gathered outside. Were we mad to continue the feast? A thrill shot through me. Excitement from toying with the forbidden. Someone handed me a goblet of wine as I joined the cluster of courtiers.

"To a hunt well hunted!" Bastian exclaimed.

"To a forest full of game." Grace joined in.

"To a long and happy reign." Ava's sweet birdsong voice chirped.

"To Mirah." Otto said quietly. "A life lost too young."

The laughter and chatter quieted and we drank solemnly. Wind whistled though the window, moaning like the gentle cry of a ghost. I shivered. The wine trickled down my throat. Bitter. Burning.

A harp strummed and Bastian drifted away to dance with his young lord. He had appeared to have given up on Otto's tragic bear eyes. Grace and Ava leaned their heads together, gossiping quietly.

Otto turned to me. "Where is Snow?"

I shrugged. "The library maybe. Or asleep."

Otto looked at me curiously. He raised his eyebrows. "You could go find her. You don't have to stay at the feast."

I shook my head. "Give her her solitude. I don't think she wants to be found." The pangs of loneliness returned in a sudden rush. Suddenly I wanted to cry. Why did she have to be like this? Why couldn't she just be happy with me? With my new home. The wine was making my mind weak. I took another sip. I shook my head. "I don't understand her sometimes."

"Isn't that part of the joy of loving someone?" Otto asked. "Letting them continue to surprise you? If you understood everything right away it would get rather dull."

I shook my head but again. It wasn't like that. It was as if she didn't even want to understand me anymore. She looked at me as if she couldn't see me.

Otto watched me as I searched my wine fogged mind for an answer. He sighed dreamily. He had that giddy expression in his eyes again. A twinkle that knew it shouldn't be there. "Love never was easy."

I looked at him curiously. "You seem to suddenly know an awful lot about love."

He blushed.

I grinned in spite of myself. "Who is she?"

He sighed again, looking miserable. "Not my bride."

I shrugged. "You're not married yet. Change your bride."

He raised an eyebrow. "And offend the Southern Ridges by sending their daughter back? King's marriages aren't that simple. It would be certain war. Besides. I've only known this girl for less than a day. How can we possibly know enough to wed one another?"

"What do you need to know? That you love her. That she loves you."

Otto shook his head. "It's not that easy."

"Pish posh." I said. "If you love this girl forget your kingdom. Forget the Southern Ridges and their prize of a daughter. I say you're a coward afraid to find a way."

I expected him to blush but instead he held my gaze with a very serious expression, stern and kingly once again. "And I say, so are you."

SNOW

I watched the courtiers dance. A dirge of death drifting through the hall. One. Five. Seven. Nine skirts twirling along with the coat tails of Bastian and his partner. They laughed and tittered while Mirah's corpse grew cold. I tried to catch Ava's eye but she, too, was dancing and laughing as if nothing had happened.

Ava.

I was beginning to realize what it was I knew. What Mirah wanted me to tell Otto.

The blood spell thrummed through my blood like a poison, surfacing with a vengeance.

Wind whistled through the broken window, carrying a flurry of snowflakes. They scattered through the hall, melting on the courters' elaborate hair dressings and velvet clothing. They kept dancing as if oblivious to the cold wind tugging at their hair and skirts.

Rose drifted past, dancing with Otto. I slunk back, careful to stay out of sight. There was no way to make them understand the urgency of discovering the truth. They were too caught up in the dance of the court to hear what little I could tell them. A dark cloud of loneliness cast over me. There was no one I could speak to. Nowhere to look for guidance.

"Ha! Fools the lot of them."

I looked down, startled. Trouble stood at my feet, watching the dance along with me.

"They do their best." I said but that didn't stop a surge of anger and frustration from running through me. How dare they dance? How dare they play act like they were hunters and ignore the darkness that needed to be hunted in their own home?

"You're crying." Trouble said.

I reached up and touched my cheeks. "I hadn't noticed."

Trouble crossed his arms, fixing me with a stare that didn't even try to look like a scowl. His brow was creased with concern. "I don't suppose you'll tell me why."

I shook my head.

"No one can help you unless you tell them how."

"I know." I said.

He shook his head, unwrapping his hands and throwing them up in the air in surrender.

I wiped my tears away with the back of my hand. He was right. I wasn't going to get anywhere standing here feeling sorry for myself. "What foods are missing from the kitchen?" I asked.

"Onions. Flour. Apples. Cinnamon. Dried figs. Salted pork. Some of everything. Why?"

"Did Sludge keep a list of exactly what went missing?"

"You bet he did. Every last ounce of flour."

"Can you get it for me?"

"Ha! You're not crying over missing flour are you?"

"No. But it's a place to start in figuring everything out."

He shrugged. "I'll fetch it."

"Thank you." I knelt down onto my knee and kissed his cheek, just above where his beard started.

He pulled away. "Get off it." He said, but I saw the hint of a smile on his face as he turned to go.

ROSE

I stared at the empty fireplace in my chamber, shivering. I'd asked Louisa not to light it. Wind howled outside. I had left the banquet after the soup course, tired from the dancing, craving the quiet, intimate company that only Snow could give but she had been nowhere to be seen. Perhaps she had decided to sleep in the library.

Or perhaps she was with Ava.

It didn't matter. Only the wind mattered. The wind that held the path back to my magic in its cries. If I could not have a quiet, intimate conversation with Snow I would have one with myself. With the wind. With the faint glowing remains of my magic.

I listened. The storm had reached its full height. It swished and swirled, howling a shrill mournful howl. Bits of snow fell through the chimney, landing in the ashes where the fire should have been. I let the blanket around my shoulders fall away, hitting the ground with a dull thud. The chamber felt like ice. My limbs were stiff from cold, protected only by my thin night shift. I closed my eyes.

Trance. Gerti had called it. I held still, falling deeper and deeper inside myself. Inside my memories. Inside my past. I had to be ready. Ready to face my nightmares.

I was in my crib in the nursery but I wasn't asleep. I banged a candlestick against the side then bit into it. It was bitter but flaked away beneath the pressure of my four teeth. I looked up.

A man cast his long, dark shadow over me. He held a shiny silver thing in his hand. It was long and pointy. Lots of men in the castle had those but I'd never tasted one before. They didn't usually bring them close enough. I reached for it.

The man pulled the shiny thing away.

I burst into tears. Why did they always take them away? It wasn't fair. I wanted to know what they tasted like.

A moment later I was in this strange man's arms, hidden inside his cloak. I stopped crying. This was alright then. I liked being held and it was warm in here. But why was I in the cloak? It must be a game! I grabbed it and tried to pull it off to surprise the man the way Nurse and brother surprised me but the man held it down. I tried again. The cloak didn't move.

It was a different game then. I kicked at him, trying to get free. Running away was a fun game too.

"Be still, child. Both our lives depend on it." His voice was gruff. Not calm and cool like Papa's but it was kind.

The man walked quickly. I liked the feeling of the quick back and forth. I closed my eyes. I could hear something else as I drifted toward sleep. Fire? Shouting?

But the man was taking me away from those things and his arms were warm and comfortable. I held still and a moment later I was asleep.

Boris didn't have to hold me still. Lucille's poison did that for him. He sprawled me over the couch and unlaced my bodice. My body lay limp and unmoving. Suddenly he was touching every inch of me. Forcefully. Ravenously. I tried to speak. To push him away. To say no. But the poison was in my blood and I could not move. He bit my nipple so hard it bled but I couldn't cry out from the force of the pain. I could feel bruises forming on my wrists. On my neck. On my thighs.

And then he had pulled up my skirt and removed his trousers and it was his flesh against mine as he bored into me, pounding and pounding and pounding. His teeth were sharp. His flesh tore at the skin inside me and I couldn't even scream.

I opened my eyes. Wind swirled in the fireplace. Tears streaked down my face. My whole body shook. Fear and anger and despair flooded my chest as I allowed the memories to sit in my mind. My shoulders shook and my eyes swelled as I cried and cried and cried, sobbing like a child into my knees. I drenched myself in all the salt water that hadn't come when I'd been locked in stillness by Lucille's poison. That I hadn't known to shed as my family had been murdered around me.

Gradually the shaking lessened. The tears still rippled down my face but they were quiet tears now instead of the big swollen sobs they had been a moment ago.

Yes, these things had happened to me.

They had hurt. They still hurt. They would always hurt.

I was still alive.

The wind outside was still howling in my ears.

I shivered from the cold bite of air brushing against my skin.

This was me. Alive.

Me.

I began to sing. Softly at first. Mournfully to match the cry of the wind. My heart drifted with the melody, still and gentle. Another drizzle of salt water trickled down my face. My voice tinkled like the ice frozen solid around my heart.

And there, crystalized inside the ice was the fire. It flickered furiously, daring the ice to hold me back. The ice melted away and the fire poured through me, warm and thick, seething like a balm against my wounds. I could feel it become one with my voice, thrumming inside my core.

I opened my eyes. A blaze crackled brightly in the fireplace. The heat flickered against the surface of my skin.

There. I'd done it. I'd used magic. I was still a witch.

I was grinning. No, laughing. The fire I had lit with my eyes flared, strong and bright.

I was still a witch.

I had always been a witch.

A witch wasn't something you could stop being.

SNOW

I went to the armory first. If I couldn't find my knife I needed a new one. The guard eyed me suspiciously as I passed him. "I'm on Otto's business." I said. "I need a knife."

He gestured toward a chest in the corner. "Otto has instructed us that you and his sister are welcome to whatsoever your heart desires." He sounded as if he didn't quite approve.

I thanked him and knelt beside the chest. It creaked as I pulled it open. The long flat surface of knife sheaths and the bent and crisscrossed shape of their knives' hilts stared up at me.

Large. Small. Thick. Thin. I pulled them out, one at a time, and removed the knives from the sheaths. The hilts rested uncomfortably in my palm. Too big. Too small. Too rough. Too heavy. They all felt wrong. I missed the familiar silver surface of the one Hans had given me. It was mine. It felt like an extension of my hand.

Twice. Three times. Four times I rummaged through the chest, trying each knife over and over, before I settled on a plain steel one with a wooden hilt. It felt strange to not have the grooves of leaf carvings scraping against my palm as I held it and it was longer than I was used to but the weight was close enough. I thanked the guard again and left.

The library was next. I needed to see the ledger book again. Mirah had wanted me to read it. I was certain that it would match Sludge's record of the stolen food.

It was cold outside. I gripped the strange new knife tightly as I made my way toward the cathedral. My eyes darted back and forth across the ward, wary of any sign of Boris. Snow fell on my hair and cloak. The wind pushed and pulled at my face and hair. I listened for a wolf's howl but only heard the icy hiss of the cold as it sang past my ears.

At last I reached the cathedral. The door opened with surprising ease. I latched it behind me and made my way across the hall toward the secret door. Melted ice dripped off of me as I wound my way up the stairs in the dark. I stopped when I reached the top. The faint glow of candlelight seeped through the half opened door. I touched the handle.

"Ava?" I pushed it open slowly. Had she left the banquet early?

A figure turned as I stepped inside. He wore a long green cloak smothered in embroidery.

"Bastian" I said, surprised. He was the last person I would have expected to leave the banquet before it had ended. I hadn't even known that the other courtiers knew about the library.

He lowered his head in a respectful bow. "Princess Snow." He winked. "Looking for a quiet place to escape the crowd, eh? This secret little library is quite ideal for that, wouldn't you say?"

"Yes." I glanced down at the book in his hand. It was small with a simple gray cover.

The ledger book.

My heart sank. "You're the last person I expected to be hiding from the crowds." I said.

Bastain placed his hand on his chest in mock indignation. "You do a charming young hooligan disservice. Even we crave the stillness of solitude from time to time." He winked again. "And my chambers seldom offer solitude."

I blushed at the implication. My eyes dropped to the book in his hand. "What is that you are reading?" I ventured cautiously.

"This?" He blinked as if he had only just noticed it. "My diary, of course. I seem to have left it here on my last visit. You must not make the mistake of giving a charming young hooligan too much credit. Solitude I crave but the vast remains of knowledge from the past?" He gestured toward the shelves of book that surrounded us then waved his hand dismissively. "I will leave that to those who care for such things. The daily dealings of my own life are a much more enduring topic."

"May . . . may I take a peak?" I asked, hoping he would be flattered not offended.

"Tisk tisk. Naughty naughty. I'm afraid it is reading not fit for the eyes of a lady such as yourself. Flattered as I am by your request, I must refuse." He yawned. "Oh my! All that riding today has left me quite weary. I will retire to my bed chamber" he winked again "and leave you free to enjoy the solitude you were seeking."

He bowed and stepped past me. I watched as he clamored his way down the staircase with the only possible hope of clarity I had clutched tight in his hands. I sat down on the bench. The cold fingers of despair gripped at my heart. How would I learn what Mirah had been trying to tell me now?

Asher. Asher would know. Would he tell me?

I could ask. I couldn't tell him how his daughter had died or ask him directly about the murder but I could ask what he knew about the smuggling. I stood up then stopped.

There was another way I could find answers. I turned and strode toward the shelf I knew it was on. I scanned across the rows of chained tomes until I found the book.

Divination.

Did I dare? Ava's magic had done nothing but fog reality. Darken it with more and more unanswered questions. I needed answers. A light to see by.

I needed to know my future.

I wasn't afraid of the changes I might find. Not anymore. What could be worse than everything I had already found in Otto's castle? Answers about what was to come, no matter how terrible, would be better than the constantly swirling swarm of questions in my head.

I opened the book, studying it carefully. The readings were complex. It took concentration to determine the right chart to use. Even choosing what question to ask was difficult. Finally I settled on one. I looked out the window at the stars. It was almost impossible to measure their location through the thick fog of the coming storm but a few of the brightest stars shone through the clouds. They were enough to sketch out a rough outline. I determined their meaning then checked the charts a second time to make sure I was right.

My blood ran cold. There were only two words written in my future. *Death*. And *Murder*.

And their source?

Me.

ROSE

It wasn't a dream. It was a nightmare. Boris dashed across the snow in his wolf form, breathing heavily as he skulked through the castle ward. He sniffed the ground, searching for flesh to sink his teeth into. He was hungry. Angry that the stupid Snow girl had escaped him. What kept calling him here? Why was he in the underworld one moment and here in this castle ward the next? He shook his head. He felt as if someone were creeping around inside his mind, watching his thoughts and it annoyed him.

His stomach growled. He caught a whiff of life a few leagues away. A goose honked.

Yes. That would do quite nicely. He crowed to himself. It had been too long since he'd had a good kill. Flesh in the underworld tasted of ash.

The geese didn't stand a chance. The pen was easy enough to jump and they had nowhere to run. He leapt in and helped himself. He had missed the sensation of warm blood drizzling down his chin. The crisp snap of a spine between his teeth. The feeling of flesh ripping beneath the force of his sharp nails. One would have been enough to satisfy his hunger but he didn't stop there. He tore into bird after bird. One flailed helplessly after its head had been removed. The living birds squawked and honked furiously until he silenced them with his teeth. Feathers flew. Bits of their flesh slid down Boris's gullet, still warm from life. If he had been in human form he would have laughed.

"Oi!" A human voice was yelling at him. A boy. "Stop that! Leave my geese alone!"

Boris ignored the voice. He tore into another bird. He felt the ribcage snap apart as he ripped it open with his claws and bit into the soft flesh in its breast.

A rock hit his nose. He turned, annoyed.

Next to the boy stood a girl with yellow hair wrapped around her head. She was a comely thing. Perhaps it would do to change form for an hour or two. He wriggled inside his flesh, glad that the moon was strong enough for him to change at will. He leapt toward her, twisting his bones midair as he shifted into human form. He felt the right parts of him harden as he pinned her to the ground.

I woke with a scream and I sat up in bed. I clasped my hand against my heart. My chest pounded like a dancer's feet.

It was just a dream. Boris was dead. Gerti and her geese were safe.

I laid down again and took deep breaths. Thump thump thump. My heart pounded as I remembered the taste of goose blood almost as if it had been in my own mouth. The rush of joy at the snapping of bones in my jaw. I shuddered and turned over then turned over again.

Embers stared at me from inside the fireplace. Shadows crawled around the faint red light in different shades of black. Soot fell from the chimney. The wind whistled outside.

Boris was dead. Why did he continue to haunt my dreams? Why did he continue to touch me against my will? The bruises he had left reached so much deeper than my skin.

Why had Snow not come to bed? I longed to curl up beside her for comfort.

The soot continued to fall inside the fireplace. Shadows echoed against shadows in the darkness around me.

I flung the blankets off and sprang to my feet. I threw Gran's cloak on over my nightshift and went to find Gerti. I shivered as I stepped outside, pulling the cloak tight around me. The wool Greta and I had spun ourselves was warm with love and memories. A comfort I needed with my heart still pounding inside my chest.

I clamored through the castle corridors and down the long winding staircase, then made my way across the hall and out into the ward. It had snowed again while I slept. The wind had stilled but the air still tasted of ice, stiffening around my nose and fingers as I made my way toward the fowlery.

I had almost reached the goose pen when I saw the first pawprints, impressed into the snow with smearings of red.

Blood.

I quickened my pace, nearing the goose pen with a wary eye. A goose honked nervously. Someone sobbed. Gray goose feathers lay strewn upon the ground. More pawprints. More blood.

The pen itself was strewn with carnage. A goose carcass with only half of its flesh gnawed off lay with its breast bones cracked open, splayed wide like fingers grasping for help. Five. Six. Nine. Thirteen more carcasses lay scattered across the pen. Each had bits of flesh ripped out of them but most of the meat had been left on their bones. Some had had their wings torn from their bodies. Others had lost their legs or their heads. Bits of their gibbets and beaks lay scattered over the ground with their blood and feathers.

Conrad stood holding the largest carcass. It had no head. He looked up when he saw me. His eyes were puffy and swollen. He wiped snot from his face with the back of his hand. "She was a good goose, Florinda. Stubborn that's all. But a good, strong goose."

Gerti stood next to him. She placed a hand on his shoulder. "She would have ended up on the king's table. This way, at least, we can bury her."

"What happened?" I asked her. But I knew. I had seen it.

"A wolf." Conrad said. "A big one. He didn't even eat them, the rotten devil. Just killed them and ruined the meat so we can't even give it to the king for his table."

"He turned into a man." Gerti said.

"A were." I said.

She nodded. "He jumped at me and turned into a man. He pinned me to the ground then disappeared. Like a ghost."

Right when I had woken. It was Boris. Somehow I had seen him in my sleep. Somehow he had crawled out of his grave to find me.

My heart quickened, pounding -no screaming- in my chest.

"I did this." I said. "I didn't mean to but . . . I did magic before I went to bed. I released my fire and this is what it did."

SNOW

The stone archway leading into the dungeon stared at me. Hungry. Inviting. I hadn't been inside a dungeon since I was a girl. Since I had hidden out of sight as Lucille had tortured a man with iron shoes.

The guards glanced at me, uncertain if they should stop me. I nodded with my most regal princess nod I could manage and lifted the lantern in my hand. "On Otto's business." I said.

They let me pass.

The corridors were dark. Still. Otto didn't have many prisoners. My footsteps echoed through the darkness like the trespasser I was.

A shadow drifted past me. Footsteps?

"Hello?"

No answer.

Iron creaked. The sound reminded me of Lucille's iron shoes. Of the scent of burning flesh. I tried not to shudder.

I lifted my lantern. Light reflected off of an empty cell with rusting iron hinges. The door was left open, casting a cross hatched shadow over the mold covered floor.

Footsteps again. Slow. Careful.

I whirled around.

The flame inside my lantern flickered. A draft drifted past me.

A presence. Near. Almost close enough to touch. And then it was gone.

Silence.

A rat perhaps.

It hadn't felt like a rat.

I moved forward again. My feet pressed against the stone floor. I was careful not to make any sound. I listened for more footsteps, gripping the new knife in my hand. The handle felt foreign. As if I were trying to protect myself with someone else's hand. The only sound I could hear was my own breathing, deep and still, as I moved past the empty cells. The dark doorways gaped at me hungrily as if longing for someone to lock within their grasp. Starved by Otto's meagre supply of prisoners.

At last I stood beside Asher's cell. His form slumped against the bars, staring out into the darkness. He did not look up nor did he turn his eyes away from the light of the lantern. I could make out the shape of his hair, casting shadows over his long nose. Something felt . . . wrong.

"Asher." I said.

No answer.

I stepped closer, holding up the lantern so I could see his face more clearly.

His mouth hung slack as if he were in shock. His eyes stared straight ahead, unseeing into the dark.

"Asher." I whispered but he did not answer. He was dead.

Like Alf. Like poor Mirah. Like Boris. Like Hans.

Like Papa.

I crouched beside the corpse and gently touched its face. Warm. Stiff. This close I could see a dribble of blood running down his neck beneath long, white hair.

A fresh kill. I reached for my knife and stood up, remembering the presence I had felt earlier.

"Bastian." My own voice reverberated back at me, growing fainter and fainter until the darkness around me echoed with the silence of a crypt. My heart thumped inside my breast. I lifted the lantern. The doors to the empty cells grinned at me with iron teeth.

If the killer was still in the dungeon there was no way for me to find them.

Something scurried across the ground. A warm, stiff touch grazed my ankle. I jumped. A rat scurried past. I looked down.

The corpse's fingers had fallen across my ankle. I stepped away, letting the fingers fall to the stone floor. I listened until the scurry of the rat's feet disappeared.

Silence.

I gripped my knife and moved forward. I could hear the swish of my skirt, the slow careful drawing of air through my lungs. The fast pattering drumbeat of my heart. I moved slowly. Alert. The lantern swung in my hand, jostling the only flicker of light in the dungeon. The cold air brushed its fingers against my neck.

I neared a turn in the corridor. The darkness was deeper here, pregnant with things unseen. The flame flickered inside my lantern, making the shadows dance.

Something scurried. Another rat. I lifted my foot and accidentally stepped down on his little animal body. He shrieked. He stood on his hind legs and bared his teeth at me. I stepped back. My foot touched something slippery.

A moment later I was picking myself up off the ground. I looked around groggily as I rose to my feet. I couldn't actually remember falling. It must have happened too fast. The rat was nowhere to be seen. The lantern lay on the ground. The light had gone out.

I felt dizzy. Had I fainted? I couldn't feel any wounds on my head from the fall.

I gripped the unfamiliar hilt of my knife and squinted into the darkness. My arm and shoulder ached from smashing against the stone. A tingling like from Ava's blood vow washed through me. I shuffled awkwardly in the darkness, making my way around the corner. A few more awkward shuffles and I could see the door leading out into the main corridor.

The corridor was dimly lit but I welcomed the low glow of lantern light as if it were a bright stream of sun. I stepped through the doorway. The guards stared at me. One reached for his sword. The other stepped forward, blocking my path.

I blinked, surprised by their behavior. Their eyes were locked on the hem of my gown. I looked down.

Blood. Bright red splattered across the white velvet. It was still wet. From when I had fallen? Or had Asher's fingers been covered in it when his corpse had touched my ankle?

I looked back up at the guards. I could see in their eyes they had no intention of letting me pass without an explanation. I needed to speak to Otto. This at least I could tell him. "Asher is dead." I said.

"Snow."

I turned. Ava was coming around the corner toward the dungeon.

"There you are, cousin. I simply must get your opinion on these silks." She placed her hand around my arm and pulled me into step with her, not even glancing at the guards. "It's foolish, I know, but I simply cannot sleep until I decide." She gripped my arm tight as she hurried along the corridor. The guards did not follow.

"Now is not the best time for silks, Ava." I said, scurrying to keep up with her long strides. Another man had just been killed. The truth needed to be told.

"Keep in step with me." Ava hissed. "My gown is covering the stain."
More loudly she said. "I can't decide if I want gold or silver for my new
curtains. How can I have my rooms ready to receive Otto after the wedding
if I can't decide on the curtains?"

ROSE

I cradled a cup of hot sage tea in my hands but I was shaking too much to drink it. Gerti sat across from me in the kitchen. It was dark but warm with only the small fire she had used to heat the kettle lit. I stared at the flames, flickering in a bright, rampant dance. Bold. Destructive.

"You can't have brought the were." Gerti said. "You can't touch our world from inside your sleep. I've heard of powerful witches talking to each other from inside their dreams but never -" She stopped suddenly. "This were. You knew him when he was alive?"

I nodded, still staring at the flames.

"Who was he?"

"He . . . ." I felt the blood leave my face. My stomach felt sick. I wanted to run. To anywhere. To everywhere. To nowhere.

"Something happened." Gerti said. "When you lost your magic. Something more than you said. It scared you from using your magic but it wants to be used. This were is the only form it knows how to take. It's trying to get your attention."

So it was true. I had done this. I had brought Boris back to life by neglecting my magic. I felt the blood leave my face. I couldn't move.

Gerti touched my arm. "Your magic brought him back, not you. It's gone rancid from being ignored. It's hurting. It's lashing out with the story you've been telling it."

I turned toward her. "I strengthened it. Before I went to bed. I let it free. Isn't that enough? Wasn't that what it wanted?" What I wanted. To light fire with my eyes again.

Gerti shook her head. "Not if you're still holding on to the fears that kept it hidden. Right now that's the only shape it knows."

Boris. That was the only shape my magic knew. How to kill. How to take.

The way I had taken the forest.

The way Boris had taken me.

My stomach swirled with sickness. He and I were the same. We shared the same greed. The same unbridled power.

Using my magic was the same as becoming him. He and my magic were the same.

Gerti touched my hand gently. "What happened?" Her tone was gentle but firm. "Why did you try to seal off your power?"

I blinked at her. I had never told anyone before. Not even Snow. She must have guessed but I'd never told her. There was no point in reliving it. In dragging out the memories when I could enjoy the day in front of me instead.

But the memories had never left my dreams and sometimes -when a man like Alf looked at me with that lustful eye or someone touched me suddenly -the memories came flooding back, overwhelming me with their power.

I looked down at Gerti's hand on mine and resisted the urge to shake her off. I closed my eyes. "His name was Boris. He killed my Gran. I forgave him for that. I thought he couldn't help it. I thought he was my friend but . . ."

There they were. The memories. Him pulling my limp legs open. The burn of his trouser string on my thighs. My body spasming outside my control.

"I couldn't move." I said. "I'd been poisoned and I couldn't move so he took what he wanted. He took what he wanted without any care for me. He told me he loved me. Over and over even while he was bruising me and tearing my flesh. He was not my friend."

I was shaking as I spoke. He was dead. He had been dead for over two years. Why did he still have so much power over me that he could make my body shake? Why wouldn't he leave my dreams alone and let me rest?

I met Geri's gaze, trying to steady myself with the warmth of her eyes. She grew distant, locked in a memory of her own. "There is nothing worse than being forced to do something against your will." She said. "No friend would do that."

"How . . ." I started then stopped. I tried again. My voice felt very small and weak. As if the tiniest breath could blow it away. "How do I untangle my magic from him? How do I take it back?"

But I knew how.

By deciding to.

By realizing that he and I were not the same. That what he had done was wrong. That I hadn't deserved it. If I had taken pieces of the forest with my power it had been to survive not for selfish pleasure.

I could never take pleasure in someone else's pain.

My power was not the same as his.

I closed my eyes. The stillness of the night echoed inside me. I shifted my position so that I was sitting straight and breathed deep. Gerti pulled her hand away from mine. My heartbeat felt slow and dull, thumping with only the faintest pulse.

But there it was. A pulse. A light. Mine. Cowering inside the darkness I had exiled it to. I breathed into it, encouraging it to grow. To expand. Coaxing it. Cherishing it. Accepting it.

Myself.

The light flickered, growing just a fraction.

Another breath. Another fraction.

It was a real flame now, flickering with a timid brightness in my breast.

I hummed softly to it, letting the music grow with the flame. The song filled me slowly, sputtering outward until it was a bonfire like the one Snow and I lit every midsummer. It roared in fury then expanded out of my control. Big. Bright. Scorching hot. Raging in every direction.

My voice faltered. It wasn't cradling a song anymore. It was holding a scream.

Another breath. Another moment of pain. Then another. Would this ever end? This raging fire. This blood curdling screech. Always in my brain. Always in my heart.

But my voice was human. It couldn't scream forever. At last I ran out of breath and the sound coming from my throat was a hum again. Soft. Calming. It pulled the fire in, tightening it into my center. No less powerful. No less strong. But contained. Still.

The song strengthened around me, echoing in my ears like wind. Only something was different. This was not Gran's song. This was mine.

It was a song made of pain and love and hope and despair. It was a song of the wood and the meadow and the stones of this castle. It was the song of a girl in love for the first time. It was the song of a woman who had learned to fear. It was the song of a child, taken from her home. It was the song of lonely, stifling nights with Greta in the village and warm cozy nights in the wood with Snow.

It was my song, bright and daring and mature. The fire burned and burned inside me. I pulled it in then out, forming it into the shape of a rose inside my breast.

Like my name.

I opened my eyes. Silence cascaded around me. Something I had not felt in years fell heavy inside me. Something strong and deep and soothing.

Peace.

SNOW

Ava whisked me into her chambers and slammed the door shut. "Now." She said. "Let's get that stain off your gown before anyone else sees it. Honestly, Snow, it's as if you are sniffing out death on purpose. Please tell me why you were coming straight out of the dungeon with blood all over your gown. And what's this?" She lifted my wrist. "Another knife? It's as if you are trying to incriminate yourself."

"Asher is dead." I said.

"I heard you tell the guards." She whisked across the room and poured water into a small basin. "You mustn't tell anyone else." She dropped a rag into the basin and pulled it out. Her tone was short and frantic. She was shaking.

A familiar tingling vibrated through my blood. The blood spell sealing another secret. "I saw Bastian in the library." I said. "He had the ledger book -the one I was looking at yesterday. Only he said it was his diary. I think he's connected to the smuggling Mirah was trying to tell me about."

Ava stared at me, puzzled. "Ledger book? I don't remember a ledger book."

I blinked. She had seen it. She had asked me if I was thinking of becoming a steward.

She tilted her head. "Are you trying to tell me that you think Bastian killed Asher?"

"No." I said, confused.

Ava's eyes sparkled in the firelight. "Because it looks very much as if you did. You were there when Alf was killed, when Mirah threw herself out the window, and now you found Asher's body in the dungeon. Never mind what you were doing there in the first place. You are the Hunter's Apprentice. Everyone knows you are a killer."

Hunter. I was a hunter.

"What reason would I have?" I asked. "What had Mirah and Asher done to me?"

"Who knows? Perhaps Mirah saw you kill Alf and told her father. You have made no secret of disliking the forester."

I opened my mouth to protest but she went on.

"Promise me you won't tell Otto about Asher, Snow, please. I won't know how to protect you."

"I already told Otto's guards. They would have seen anyways. Doesn't it look worse if I try to hide something I didn't even do?" I was beginning to grow tired of her secrets. Her insistence on hiding. Was it me she wanted to protect or herself?

Ava closed her eyes as if in pain. "You naive child. Do you really think Otto will protect you after you jilted him for his sister?"

I stared at her. Did she know Otto so little? I might be a killer but I wasn't a murderer. He knew that. He was my friend. My choice not to marry him did not change that.

There was a knock at the door. Ava rose to open it. Feet clattered as Otto stepped inside. Glen, Trouble's eldest brother, and a handful of guards followed. Otto held out his hand. He uncurled his fingers to reveal a long silver object carved with vines.

"My knife." It was all I could do not to reach out and snatch it.

"We found this outside the window next to Mirah's chamber where Alf was killed." Otto said. "How did it get there?"

I blinked at him. My stomach turned with nausea. I opened my mouth to speak but the familiar tingling and dizziness permeated my body. No sound came out. Unspoken words screamed like a pain inside my brain.

What would I say even if I could speak? That I had found Alf's body and hidden it from him? That I had been so afraid of being accused that I had thrown my knife out the window even though I was innocent?

I turned toward Ava with pleading eyes. There must be something she could do. A way to release me from the blood vow. Even the weak defense of the truth was better than this terrible silence.

Ava's eyes strayed down to the edge of my gown. The blood had begun to dry, turning a deep burnt orange. Like fire. Like rusted gold.

Otto followed her gaze. He creased his brows and looked back up at me. His eyes filled with concern. "You can tell me the truth, Snow. I will believe you.""

I opened my mouth again. No sound came out. It hung open, dazed and stupid. A fresh wave of dizziness swept through me and I had to step back to keep from falling over.

Otto held my gaze. "Snow," he said, more slowly this time "the guards tell me you went to see Asher in the dungeon. Why?"

Dizziness. Nausea. Tingling through my whole body. Like bee stings. Like needles. I struggled to concentrate. The room began to swim around me. I reeled in confusion.

"Snow," Otto said. "Asher's body was found in his cell. Newly killed. Tell me what happened."

I clutched my head, struggling to stay upright as the truth I had begun to suspect struck me clear as ice, harsh and indisputable.

Ava had whisked me up here just as I had been going to tell the guards about the body. She had been the one to insist I throw my knife out the window. She had enacted the blood vow. To protect me? No. To incriminate me.

It wasn't Otto and his court I couldn't trust. It was Ava. It was the blood vow. It was my own silence.

No more silence then. Vow or no vow, I would speak. Somehow, despite the magic, I would find my voice. I would tell Otto the truth.

A scream erupted from my throat. My whole body began to shake as the sound made its way out of my lungs, failing to form into words. My throat felt as if a knife were stuck in it. Saliva built up in my mouth and drizzled down my chin, forming a slimy, bubbling foam.

"She's gone mad!" Ava exclaimed.

As if to confirm her words my scream transformed into shouts of gibberish. Loud, driveling sounds with no meaning hickuped out of my mouth. If I concentrated just a little harder I could shape them into words. I could make everything make sense. I could be heard.

My body ceased shaking and began to convulse. What was it I needed to say again? It didn't matter. I just needed to say it. The room swam around me. Blackness. A scream in my brain. More blackness. Sound. I needed to speak.

Someone shouted. Hands grabbed at my arms as they flailed against my will. I was on the ground now. My nails scraped against flesh as someone tried to hold me still.

More blackness. More screaming. Speak. I needed to speak. Blackness. A scream in my brain. Blackness.

Nothing.

Screaming.

Nothing.
Speak.
Speak.
Speak.
Nothing.

ROSE

Gerti and I stepped out of the kitchen. The night was still, covered in what was now a thick blanket of snow. The storm clouds had cleared, showcasing a beautiful crescent moon. It glowed bright and vibrant like the fire burning in my core. I shivered and pulled Gran's cloak tighter around my shoulders. The shadows of the stone ovens stood in front of us. Still. Asleep.

"Is that Otto?"

I glanced in the direction she had indicated before I realized she hadn't said 'King' Otto.

Otto came slowly into view. His face was pale and drawn. His eyes wide and worried. He stopped when he reached us. His eyes drifted to Gerti in surprise. "Gerti." He said.

A soft smile played on her lips. "Hello." She said. I realized all at once where I had heard the song Otto had been whistling earlier. It was the same strange eerie melody Gerti had been humming from home. Like the dance of the dead. Was she the girl he had fallen in love with so suddenly?

Otto shook himself. He blinked and turned toward me. "I arrested Snow."

My heart froze. "What?" I demanded, no longer interested in Otto's sudden romance. "On what grounds?"

Otto ran his hand through his hair. "Asher's Murder. And Alf's. Maybe Mirah's"

"That's ridiculous." A flame sparked inside one of the stoves. My magic, reacting to my anger.

Otto lifted his hands helplessly. "Her knife was found outside Mirah's window and she was seen leaving the dungeon with blood on her gown. As the upholder of the law I am a slave to it. I cannot make exceptions. But that's not all Rose. She's . . . she's rabid."

"Rabid?"

"She started writhing. Foaming at the mouth. It took two guards to restrain her."

Gerti gasped.

"She's gone mad." Otto said. "Perhaps it was the madness that did the killing."

"No." I said. She couldn't be mad. Not my Snow. Not my sweet, strong, brave Snow. I had to go to her. Now. I turned toward the door.

A hand touched my shoulder. Gerti. I turned to shake her off but her still, brown eyes stopped me. She blinked, pregnant with thought. "Have you ever wanted to tell someone something but couldn't"

"No." I said. ."I always say what I'm thinking."

"Then you are very fortunate." She blinked again. Twice. Once at me and once at Otto. His gaze lingered on her. "Sometimes" She said. Deliberately. Slowly. Pronouncing her words as if they were made of lightning that might strike her if she misspoke. "When a secret wants to come out but I can't tell anyone I talk to the stoves." She glanced at the big domed brick structures in front of us.

I stared at her, then I glanced at Otto. He was watching Gerti with a faint twinkle of understanding in his eyes. "Is now one of those times?"

Gerti gazed back at him. Her hand weighed down on my shoulder. "Stoves are very good listeners."

"I need to talk to Snow." I shook her hand away and turned toward the keep. Otto followed me around the corner of the kitchen. Our feet crunched into the snow.

Rabid. How could Snow be rabid? I remembered the dark look in her eyes as she had stared into the woods on the hunt that afternoon. How angry she had been trying to tell Otto . . . something. About Asher. About smuggling. *It's dangerous here* she had told me but I hadn't listened.

Otto touched my arm. "Wait." He pulled me back against the wall to the kitchen and placed his finger over his lips. "Listen."

I leaned against the wall. The stone was cold. I listened.

Nothing.

I moved to go. We were wasting time.

Otto grabbed my wrist. "Wait." He mouthed, insistent.

Gerti's footsteps pattered against the snow. Lightly. Carefully. The wind whistled through the ward. The moon glowed up ahead. Finally she spoke, strong and clear, addressing the stoves.

AVA

First, my name is not Gerti. It is Ava. Princess Ava.

Gerti and I were friends. At least, I had always thought that we were. We were girls together. Sisters almost. The rest of the court might have seen her as my handmaid but to me she was Gerti. My best friend. My confidant. My riding companion and the best at blind man's bluff out of anyone I had ever known. Perhaps because she could be so quiet. So agile. So observant. We studied together and played pranks on our tutors together. We went on boat rides together and spied on the grown up courtiers from inside cupboards. At night she brushed my hair and mended my clothes. It never once occurred to me that she might resent it. It never occurred to me that it bothered her that at our first ball I had worn layers of gold silk and she had worn a simpler gown made from rich, green wool.

It never occurred to me when Mother told me to tell no one the secrets of shade magic that she could have meant Gerti. I told Gerti everything. I told her the way my heart pattered when I spoke to the stable boy. I told her that I dreamed almost every night that I was the wind. I told her when I had first began my monthly bleeding. Why shouldn't I tell her about blood vows and blood children and how one must be very careful about using the spells of shade magic even on oneself because they were unbreakable? Gerti listened, sympathetic as always. Keen. Observant. Understanding.

I had just turned sixteen when my father told me that King Otto of the north was to be my husband. I was pleased. My mother had been betrothed to him when she was young and had always spoken very well of him. "He is kind." She told me "He will treat you well." My father was happy to be making such a good alliance with the northern kingdom and perhaps equally as pleased to see that Otto would be married quickly now that he had returned. Before he had an occasion to see Mama again because it was rumored that he had somehow remained young and handsome despite his years and Mama loved to tell stories of him. How they had hunted together as children. How they had stolen sweets from the kitchen and watched dancing bears.

Gerti listened to all the stories with me, squealing with glee at my good fortune not to be sent to the emperor across the ocean who was twice my father's age. There was no question that Gerti would come with me to the north. She was the first of my escort chosen and I was eager to share this journey with her. My comforter. My protector. The one person who could always make me laugh. I would never have dared make a new home for myself without her.

The preparations to leave did not last long. It was a long journey over a harsh terrain and a large caravan would have slowed us down. Father chose two of his best guards to accompany Gerti and I and I spent one last autumn at home while Mother helped me choose my dowry.

Mother wept when she finally said farewell. I stood with her and Father outside the castle gate. She held me close and pressed a handkerchief into my hand. I looked down. It had three drops of my blood stained onto the silk.

"Yours." Mama whispered. "Arrive at Otto's castle safely. I command it."

Shade magic. It was the first time I had ever seen it practiced. I tucked the handkerchief safely in my sleeve.

Along with Gerti and Papa's guards I brought Falada, the horse I had had since childhood. He was not young but still strong enough for the journey. I enjoyed feeding him and grooming him myself each night as I had never been allowed to do in the castle.

The first few weeks went peacefully enough. Leon and Jonas were strong, steady guides. Leon hardly spoke at all. Jonas never stopped babbling. Trudging through the wilderness was so very different than life in Father's castle. It was hard at first. Colder. More tiring. I adjusted soon enough. Gerti always had a game to play or a story to tell for the long rides. One day we whistled every time Jonas spoke of dice games. Another day we named the cobblestones in the river and made up long tales about them.

Things became more difficult when we reached the mountains. The climb was steep and difficult for the horses. We had to dismount and lead them through the pass.

"We're close." Jonas kept saying. "Only a few more days and we'll be feasting once more. Do you suppose Otto's guards will play dice?""

Ava whistled.

There was a storm halfway up the pass. Rain poured down on our faces and the already harsh terrain grew wet with mud. I slipped. My foot hovered over the edge of the cliff. Leon rushed to pull me and Florinda to safety. We pulled ourselves away from the edge and I clutched Gerti in relief.

"We'll rest a moment." Jonas said. "Catch our breath before moving on."

The stones above us rumbled. Jonas looked up. Leon shouted. Someone pushed me out of the way just as a slide of rocks crashed down over the path. Jonas, Leon, and both their horses tumbled over the side. I watched them fall, cold with shock, as an avalanche of stones tumbled after them. My eyes filled with dust, dampened by the rain.

Gerti clutched me tight. She was shaking. I held her close as the rocks kept falling and falling. At last they stopped. We were both covered in mud.

"What will we do now?" Gerti asked me. "We have no protection. There will be robbers. Thieves. Who will catch us if we start to fall again? How will we find our way?"

I was shaking almost as much as her but I steadied myself. I took the handkerchief Mama had given me out of my sleeve and showed her the drops of blood. "Mama gave this to me. This is my blood. She commanded me to arrive at Otto's castle alive."

Gerti gasped. "Shade magic."

I nodded.

Her face darkened. Rain streaked down her mud coated face. "It will only protect you."

I shook my head. "Do you think I would continue the journey without you? I will tie you to me if I have to to make sure we reach the castle together."

We huddled together that night, holding each other close as the storm raged around us. When morning came we packed up the supplies that had not tumbled over the cliff with Leon and Jonas and continued on our way. My entire dowry was gone.

The main path was blocked by the landslide so we had to backtrack to find another one. We made our way up the mountain and then down it again with no idea if we were going the right way. Another rockslide almost hit us but we managed to pull back in time and it was small enough that we could make our way around it without finding a new path.

At last we reached flat ground. The mountain terrain gave way to a thick forest. We trotted beneath the trees, looking for any sign of where we were.

It was only a few hours before we came upon a forester. He was stooped next to a river getting a drink of water. I called out to him.

"I am Princess Ava." I said. "Which direction is King Otto's castle? I am to be his bride."

The forester stood. He looked at my mud soaked gown then at Gerti, then at our horses, then at me again. Finally he bowed. "Then you will soon be my queen." He said. "I am King Otto's own forester. His castle is a day and a half's journey along this path. I would offer to escort you there myself but you will be much faster on horseback than I will be on foot."

I thanked him, unable to believe our luck. I knew it was the doing of the handkerchief in my sleeve. Only magic could have led us to our destination so easily.

The forester faded into the woods and we stopped at a stream to let Falada and Gerti's mare drink.

I stroked Falada's soft, warm neck as he drank, comforting him, thanking him for carrying me all this way. Then I stooped to my knees to take a drink myself.

The water was cold like ice as I dipped my hands in and lifted it to my lips. I drank greedily despite the cold, letting the liquid refresh me from the inside out. I reached for a second draught but I moved too quickly. My handkerchief fell out of my sleeve. The water thinned the deep brown blood stains as it swept along with the current.

"Quick!" I cried to Gerti She stood downstream splashing water on her face. "Mama's handkerchief!"

Gerti was quick. She stepped forward, splashing her foot into the water as she snatched the handkerchief up in her hand. She stood, staring at it in her palm as if in a trance. Finally she looked up at me. She smiled. Playful. Mischievous. Like she did when she had a new idea for a game.

I stood, grateful, as always, for her prompt and willing action.

Gerti's smile deepened. "Touch your nose." She said.

I touched my nose.

Gerti giggled. "Twirl."

I twirled obediently. "Gerti" I smiled in spite of myself. "Please don't."

"Be quiet."

I blinked. It was one thing to play at making me dance. It was another to take away my voice. I looked at her meaningfully and held out my hand.

"Don't call me Gerti." She said. "Call me Ava. Call me Princess Ava."

"Princess Ava," I said. "Please give me back my handkerchief."

"No." She stuck it in her pocket. "I am going to keep it. Never tell anyone about it. Never tell anyone that I used to be called Gerti. Tell everyone that you are called Gerti and that I am the southern princess, Ava. Never tell anyone what is happening now. When we arrive at King Otto's castle tell him that I am Princess Ava. I will be his bride, not you."

Each command hit me like a cold wind. This had to be a game. One of Gerti's clever games. She was my friend. She would never take my name and my past and my future from me all at once. Where was the game? What cleverness was I missing?

"Why?" I asked. She would tell me. She would tell me and it would make sense. It was a riddle I didn't know the answer to yet. That was all. Gerti was my friend. My best friend.

Gerti laughed. Her voice sounded like bells tinkling in my ears. "Why do you think? I want to be a princess. No, I want to be a queen. I want to wear the best gowns. I want to snap my fingers and have people fetch and carry for me."

She meant it. She was taking my life from me. I swallowed. "All you had to do was ask." I said. "I would have given you whatever gowns you wanted."

"It's not the same." She said. "I don't want borrowed power. I want my own. I want power over you like you've always had over me."

That was when I realized that all of our days together. All of our games and secrets. They had been a chore to her. Nothing more.

The remaining part of the journey seemed to last forever. We rode in silence as the wind seeped into my bones. I closed my eyes and let it dance in my soul, a slow, mournful dance, dark like the night. The wind at least had not abandoned me. I hummed a song from home, lively but mournful. Like the dance of the dead.

Dusk came and we made camp. I did not sleep. When I could hear Gerti snoring gently on the other side of the fire I rose and stood over her. I held a small carving knife in my hand.

One slice. One slice across the throat and she would die.

I could kill her but I could never tell anyone who I was unless she told me to. If I arrived at King Otto's castle alone I would still have to tell them my name was Gerti. They would turn me away if I didn't have the 'princess' with me.

Could I go home? They would know me there but I could never tell them why I had returned or why I called myself Gerti. A piece of who I was would still be missing from me.

If I could go home at all. Mother's command to arrive at King Otto's castle alive still hung over me.

No. Staying with Gerti, hoping she would change the command, was my best chance.

Besides. I didn't want to kill Gerti. My chest ached with the loss of what I had thought I had had.

I left Gerti and went to stand by Falada. I stroked him gently first to wake him, then quieted him so that he would not wake Gerti.

"I'm sorry." I whispered and sliced a small cut on his withers. He whinnied in pain. I let three drops of his blood drop onto my skirt. "Speak."

I commanded him. "Speak for me in the language of men until I can speak for myself."

"If your mother only knew. Her heart would break in two." He said in a reedy nasally voice not meant for human speech.

I jumped, startled by the strangeness of it.

Something stirred behind me. I turned to see Gerti standing on her feet. She looked at Falada, frightened, then looked at me. She looked at the knife in my hand. The cut on his withers.

"It won't work." She clutched the handkerchief tightly in her hand. "Go back to sleep." She commanded." Do not go home."

I obediently laid down and went to sleep.

That next day as we traveled closer and closer to the castle Falada spoke every few hours.

"If your mother only knew, It would break her heart in two."

Every time he spoke Gerti looked a little paler. It wasn't what I'd hoped he would say but it would be hard to explain to King Otto. A bud of hope sprouted in my breast. If she couldn't explain it perhaps the truth would surface and if Otto learned the truth he could force her to change her commands. I hummed as we continued our journey, enjoying the sun as it shone over the mountains.

A few miles from the castle Gerti stopped. She found some large stones and pounded them onto Falada's hoof until his bone cracked.

I screamed from my place on the saddle and leapt onto the ground. Gerti held up the handkerchief. "Stop." She said. "Tell no one what I have just done."

We walked the rest of the way, leading Falada as he trotted after us on a broken leg. He whinnied with pain at each step. The shrill, panicked sound vibrated through me, echoing like the wind in my soul.

The hope in my breast shriveled and fell apart like ash. I had done this to him. I had tried to use him to save myself and now every step he took was agony.

Gerti told the guards at Otto's castle that Falada had fallen and broken his hoof and needed to be released from his pain. I didn't argue. I couldn't bear to see him suffer anymore.

The guards brought out an ax when we reached the inner ward. Gerti went into the keep but I stayed and watched as they hacked off my best friend's head, one messy unfinished blow at a time. He shrieked in pain with the unearthly voice I had commanded him to speak with. A scream that was almost human filled the ward.

I didn't cry. My face should have been wet with tears but it wasn't. I was too hollow inside. There was nothing in there but dry air.

The guards cleaned off the ax and began to clear away Falasa's carcass. Wind whistled through the ward. A dry, wheezy voice spoke.

"If your mother only knew. Her heart would break in two"

The guards dropped Falada's head. They stared at each other in horror.

I ran to Falada and knelt by his head. I felt his muzzle. He had no breath -no warmth of blood beneath his skin -but he stared at me with eyes that saw. I cradled him in my lap and the tears came.

I had cursed him. Even in his death he was compelled to speak for me. His pain would never end until he I could speak for myself again.

I refused to let the guards bury his head. His eyes still saw. I would not condemn them to stare at darkness for eternity.

I did not want to work as Gerti's handmaid so I asked what other jobs needed to be done in the castle. The guards told me I could help the boy

Conrad with the geese. The next morning we went out to the meadow with the noisy flock of birds. I took Falada's head with me and put it on a pike along our path so that I would see him everyday. So that he would remind me not to adjust to my new life. So that I would remember that he Conrad with the geese. The next morning we went out to the meadow with the noisy flock of birds. I took Falada's head with me and put it on a pike along our path so that I would see him everyday. So that he would remind me not to adjust to my new life. So that I would remember that he was in pain and find a way to release myself from Gerti's shade magic so I could release him from mine.

ROSE

Gerti -no Ava -stopped speaking. I peaked over Otto's shoulder. She was staring at the shadows inside the unlit stove in front of her. Wind stirred the ashes, swirling them inside the brick dome.

Otto stepped away from the protection of the kitchen wall. "Princess Ava."

She turned toward him. Her eyes were wide and still. She clasped her hand to her heart.

Otto met her gaze. A slow smile spread across his face. Neither boyish nor kingly. Ruggish. Handsome. "You are Princess Ava."

Ava smiled back, open and brisk like a storm. It began on her lips then cascaded up to her eyes and nose and cheeks like the bright brush of morning. She nodded. "Yes." It was a whisper, clear and soft in the darkness. She gasped then touched her mouth as if she didn't know what it was. "It worked. The blood command is broken. I didn't know if it would work. I didn't even know if you would listen."

"That's why it worked." Otto gazed at her as if she might suddenly fly away. An odd mixture of glee and awe bubbled in his eyes. "You didn't know we were listening so you were able to speak but, without knowing it, you disobeyed your handmaid's commands."

"I thought all blood spells were irreversible." Ava laughed. The joy in her smile burned through her eyes. "I am Ava." She said then laughed again.

"Ava." Otto repeated the name. "My betrothed."

"Otto." I touched his arm lightly to bring him back to reality. "You said Snow was foaming at the mouth, trying to speak." I recalled the secret glances I had seen between her and the false Ava in the ward and shuddered. "Could she be under a blood command as well?"

Otto blinked. He turned toward me. Realization dawned in his eyes.

"Take me to her cell." I demanded.

SNOW

Nightmares scurried in my brain like rats. Giant, hungry rats. The kind that gnawed on your flesh while you slept.

Papa stared at me with holes for eyes.

Lucille pointed at me with her soft, elegant finger.

Me.

I had done this.

I tried to speak. To explain that I hadn't meant to but my voice was gone. I gagged then choked, trying to make sound come out of my throat but nothing would come. It had dried up like an old well.

Then came the screams.

Papa screaming in his sleep as the poison took him.

The man in Lucille's dungeon screaming as he danced in her iron shoes.

A little girl screaming in a tower at night where no one could hear while Hans harvested her heart for Lucille's dinner table.

Hans' screaming eyes as Boris sliced his throat.

Rose screaming in her sleep as she relived memories she had never dared tell me of over and over and I could do nothing to protect her.

Mirah, screaming at me to save her father. To speak. To tell the world what I knew. To believe my own doubts.

Each scream pounded into my brain. Like an anvil. Like a deep knife thrust. My head ached with the sound but I could not speak. I could not find the words. To warn them. To stop them.

My silence had destroyed so much.

I opened my eyes and stared into darkness. My head ached. I was laying on the ground. It was hard. Stone. I groaned and sat up. A rat scurried past. It was an ordinary rat. Not large enough to eat my flesh. The air smelled dank and stale.

The dungeon. I was in the dungeon. Did I remember being brought here? Everything was so muddled. All I knew was that I needed to speak.

"Stand up."

Ava's voice.

I stood up.

"Touch your nose."

I touched my nose.

She laughed. A giddy, giggly laugh as if she were a child discovering a new game. "Now dance."

I wove first in one direction then the other. I spun then bounced. My feet moved as if they had a mind of their own, mimicking the steps Dana and Elise had taught me. My heart quickened in my chest. My feet grew sore. My side ached from so much motion but still I danced and danced and danced.

Ava's laughter echoed off the dungeon walls, creating a light bubbly rhythm for my feet. She clapped her hands together in excitement. "How does it feel, princess, to be a servant? A slave to someone else's whims?"

"What did you do to me?" I demanded. I stepped to the side and spun in a circle.

I could see her now in the shadows, gazing at me from outside my cell. She held up a handkerchief smeared with blood. "You should never have let me touch your blood. Vow of silence? That wasn't half of it. I could have commanded you to kill Asher yourself if I'd have wanted to. I told you to forget what you saw instead."

That was how I'd got blood on my gown then.

"Stop dancing. You're making me dizzy." She stuffed the handkerchief back into her pocket and pulled out a ring of keys. She jingled them in the air. "I've come to let you out. We're friends after all, aren't we?" She inserted the key into the lock. A hollow click echoed through the dungeon and the door fell open with a long, ominous squeak.

I stared at her. "What game are you playing? This isn't a play to be acted out for your amusement."

"Isn't it though? Aren't others always ordered around for the amusement of those with power? We memorize our lines and we play our parts but no one cares who we are underneath all that show."

I stared at her. Court did sometimes feel like a whir of gossip and finery where everyone spoke and no one listened. A shallow dance where everyone was expected to perform for the amusement of others. "You're wrong." I said. "They do care. They don't always see but when they do see they care."

She laughed again. "Spoken like a born princess, defending her kind. I thought I wanted to be like you. I thought I wanted to be a princess and marry the king. I wanted to be the golden girl for once -the special one - instead of Ava. But Otto's brute of a forester saw Ava and I when we were traveling. He recognized me. I told him if he told Otto who I was I would tell him that he and Bastian were smuggling but he laughed at me. He said the king wouldn't care about smuggling when he realized some common bitch was trying to sneak into his bed. I was only going to take his blood at first. To command him to be silent. But the bastard deserved to die. I went for his throat instead of his hand.

"Be like you?" She laughed. Frantically. Manically. Her eyes widened almost as if she were frightened as she giggled like a child. "Never if it means turning a blind eye to rot like him. Poor Mirah. I really did want to protect her but she saw Alf and I struggling. I had to keep her quiet. I didn't realize she would fight so hard to save her father.

"Still. It could have stopped there if you hadn't insisted on speaking to Asher. He didn't know the truth. He thought Mirah had killed Alf but you knew that she didn't. If she had she would have confessed herself instead of throwing herself off the staircase to get your attention. You would have kept digging for answers and Asher would have had no reason to be silent once he knew his daughter was dead. Shade magic is more difficult than I had expected it to be. Like Ava, you might have found a way to speak. The easiest way to silence you and Asher was for one of you to die and the other to be accused."

"Then why come let me out?" I asked. "Why tell me any of this?"

She sighed heavily and blinked at me with the pained expression of a martyr. "Ava -the real Ava - broke the command of silence I put on her. God knows how but she told Otto who I am and he doesn't want to marry me anymore."

"He never wanted to marry you." I reminded her.

"Be quiet." She held up the handkerchief. Her eyes flashed with anger. With pain and -for the tiniest fraction of a second - with fear. Her hand was shaking. "You will do something for me that will distract the court from anything a stupid little goose girl tries to tell them. Kill him, Snow. Kill Otto."

I shook my head. "It won't work. Rose will still believe her."

"Oh?" Ava -or whoever she really was -asked mockingly. "And who will believe Rose? The lover of the king's murderer. No doubt you thought she would take the throne after he died but she won't. She'll be burned as a witch like the old days and the throne will be given to the king's betrothed. I don't care how many of you stupid royals have to die. I will never go back to being a servant. Never." She stopped shaking and glared at me defiantly. She lifted her hand and uncurled her fingers around a long, silver item, deadly and elegant.

My knife.

"Take it." She said.

I obeyed. The familiar groove of the hilt felt comfortable in my palm. I gripped it tight, almost feeling safe.

"Kill Otto." She repeated. "Kill Otto and anyone who tries to stop you. Now."

"No." I said but I was powerless to resist the command. I lifted one foot and then the other as if I were a puppet on strings. Her eyes lit up in the darkness as she watched me. I stepped out of the cell and moved past her out into the corridor. I didn't know where Otto was but my body didn't care. It lurched forward with a will of its own.

I seethed with anger. How dare Otto invite us here. How dare he entice us from our happy cottage with the charms of his castle only to be trapped in these halls of death and corruption. I had tried to warn him. To tell him something was wrong but he was deaf to my concerns. Hatred seethed inside me. White like ice. Hot like fire.

No. I struggled to reign in my thoughts. Let False-Ava control my body if she must but my thoughts -my mind -was my own. I wouldn't surrender those to the shade magic.

My heart ached with the pain of betrayal. False-Ava's betrayal for using my blood to control me. Otto's betrayal for locking me away. For not believing that I was innocent.

Rose's betrayal for not seeing how much I needed her. For wanting to keep me in a place that brought me so much pain.

A rat scurried across my path. I flung my knife at him with a quick flick of the wrist. The blade sliced through his ribs, stopping him in his tracks. He squeaked in pain then fell, lifeless, onto the stone. I stooped and pulled out the blade. His legs flailed then he was still.

Kill Otto and anyone who tries to stop you. The command buzzed in my head. The beast had made the mistake of stepping into my path. I stepped past the carcass and moved forward. My feet echoed in the darkness as they pattered against the stone. I plunged my way through the corridor and towards the dungeon entrance.

"Princess Snow." A guard stood in front of me as I reached the door, blocking my path. He was the same one who had let me out my first morning in the castle. The one with curly brown hair and deep blue eyes.

I blinked at him. "Don't try to stop me." I pleaded.

The guard straightened. His lips pressed together in a firm line. He placed his hand on his sword hilt. I could see a hint of fear creeping into his deep blue eyes. Or was it regret? "Go back to your cell." He commanded. "This is Otto's business."

I stepped toward him, ignoring his command. My blood buzzed with the force of False-Ava's control.

"Stop." He drew his sword.

My hand raised and took aim. The blade of my knife sang through the air. It landed in the center of his throat. Blood drenched the black of his tunic. It splattered over my chin and into my mouth. The guard spasmed, then lurched, staggering backwards. His deep blue eyes blinked at me in surprise as he toppled forward. His skull cracked against the ground.

I reached to pull my knife out of his throat. His body jerked back almost as if it still had the touch of life in it. I stared at him, shocked by what I had done.

A killer they had called me. A murderer.

Now it was true.

Two more guards rushed toward me as I stepped out into the corridor. Their swords were already drawn.

Was there a chance they would kill me or would False-Ava's command ensure that I lived until it was obeyed?

The guards reached me. I hoped they could stop me. I hoped they could save Otto.

A dodge. A step to the side. I swayed easily out of the line of their sword blades. The three of us moved in a strange macabre dance. The quickness of my motions was inhuman, my body a slave False-Ava's command. A moment later my knife was digging into one of their chests. He cried out, coughing up blood. I grabbed his sword from his hands, holding it out just as his companion came at me from the other side. It sliced through the top of his shoulder, lodging downward into his chest. The two men toppled over together.

My heart pounded in my chest. My breath was short, fluttering like a butterfly's wing in my lungs. Were they dead? Was stopping them enough or did they have to die?

Kill Otto. False-Ava's command echoed in my mind. *Kill Otto and anyone who tries to stop you.* I could already see the life fading from their eyes as they moaned in pain. Anyone who tried to stop me would die. Anyone who tried to touch me. I would kill them. False Ava had commanded it.

I retrieved my knife. The blood smeared onto my hands and gown. The velvet had more brown and red than white now. I stood and moved past their spasming bodies.

I made my way through the rest of the castle in silence. A few nobles peeked their heads down from the stairs. Servants scurried out of the way. I closed my eyes, thanking the God from the priests' talks. Please let there be no more blood. Don't let anyone else try to stop me.

A gust of cold wind met me as I stepped out into the ward. The slightest hint of dawn had begun to brighten the sky.

"Snow."

Trouble's voice.

No.

I turned.

No.

He stood with his arms crossed. He glared at me with a genuine fury that I had never seen in him before. "You're a devil of a mess." He said. "Do you care to tell me why you're covered in blood?"

"I . . . . can't." I said.

"You can."

"Trouble. Please." I whispered.

He reached into his coat pocket and pulled out a piece of parchment smothered with ink. "Glen had a scribe write down everything Sludge is missing from the kitchen like you asked." He dropped the parchment down at my feet. "Now, tell me exactly what is going on, Snow." He pulled out his pipe and reached for his flint.

No.

False-Ava's command buzzed through me. I tried to fight against it. To hold my body still.

Kill.

No. I could step around him. He hadn't tried to stop me yet. Not really. I stepped to the side.

Trouble dropped his pipe and followed the step, blocking my path.

No.

It was quick. As painless as I could make it. A swift slice across the throat where the blood would drain the fastest. I felt cold as I watched him fall. Cold as if it were my own blood draining into a pool on the stone ground. Cold and empty and still.

No.

Would there be anything left of me when this was done? Would I collapse and die of pure exhaustion once Otto was dead?

I hoped so. There would be no life to return to. Not after this.

"Snow."

It was Otto's voice this time. I closed my eyes in relief. I would kill him. I would kill him quickly and this nightmare would be over. I would be free.

"Snow. What have you done?"

Rose's voice.

"He's gone." I said without turning. My voice was stiff and leaden, weighed down with defeat. With horror. With grief. "Don't let anyone else try to stop me, Otto. Please. Only you have to die."

"No." A girl's voice. Someone I didn't know. Brisk like the wind.

"Don't be stupid." Rose said. "No one has to die."

"She commanded you to kill me." Otto said.

"Yes." I turned. My hand had already lifted, gripping my knife hilt as I prepared to take aim. "You and anyone who tries to stop me." I repeated Ava's words, hoping he would understand what they meant. That I couldn't be stopped. That anyone who tried would die.

Otto met my gaze. His eyes grew quiet. He understood. His lips quirked into a half smile. "There was a time I was certain you would be the death of me. I thought it was just an expression."

Tears welled in my eyes. My hand shook. His eyes were so gentle. Peaceful. I opened my mouth to take it back. To tell him that his armies could stop me. That they had to at least try. Better they all die than him. Our red bear. Our brother.

"No one try to stop her." Otto commanded. Guards and servants had begun to gather around us in the ward. Whispers rustled through the early morning cold.

"Rose," Otto continued in his loud, clear king's voice. "you are unquestionably my heir. You will rule when I am gone." He touched the hand of the golden haired girl beside him. Was she the goose girl I had met my first morning in the castle? "Ava." His voice softened. "I love you. I would have been honored to have you as my queen. You will have a home here in my castle for as long as you wish it."

"No." The girl said. Pleadingly. Furiously. Wind stirred in the ward, fingering furiously through our hair. "Otto, the commands can be disobeyed. I proved that. We will find another way."

Kill. Kill. Kill. A wave of nausea swept through me. I couldn't hold back anymore.

"I won't buy my life with the lives of my subjects." Otto said. "No one else will die. No one but me."

Kill. Kill. Kill.

"Snow." Rose said. "You don't have to kill anybody. Ava broke Gerti's hold on her. You can too."

I couldn't hold back my hand any longer. My knife was aimed for his neck. Another quick death. As painless as I could make it.

Otto closed his eyes, bracing himself for what was to come.

A weight slammed into me, knocking me to the ground. My shoulder smacked hard against the stone. I rolled over to see who was on top of me.

Except that I would recognize her touch anywhere. The wild elegance of her movements as she pinned me to the ground.

No.

"Rose." Otto shouted. "You idiot. Now both of us will die

Rose reached for my knife. I stopped struggling for just a moment as I met her gaze. Her hazel eyes flared with determination.

"I won't let you." She said. "I won't let you kill him."

Her death sentence.

I closed my eyes. My whole body went cold. Limp. My blood felt like ice. Not Rose. Please, not Rose. Anybody but my Rose.

Rose held my gaze. She held me still against the ground. "You can stop this, Snow." Her voice was soft, warm and soothing like an embar. No judgement. No condemnation for all that I had just done. For what I was about to do. Just the gentle glow of understanding. "This isn't you, Snow. Command or no command, you can stop it. Find a way."

But there wasn't a way. Against my will I had begun to struggle again. I was small but my limbs were strong from hunting. From climbing. From chopping wood.

And I knew Rose's body.

I knew that she was the most sensitive on the inside of her left knee. I knew that she would twitch if I touched the right side of her neck. I knew that one hip couldn't twist as far as the other one.

Rose knew my body too. She knew that my left elbow was stiff. She knew that it was my instinct to jump whenever someone touched my throat.

We struggled together on the cold stone, locked in a grapple so intimate that it almost felt like making love. We writhed together with the rhythm of my heartbeat, pulsing loud like an executioner's drum as I prayed and prayed that I would lose.

I couldn't lose. False-Ava's command forbade me too. I could have been wrestling a giant and I would have overcome it. I struck the inside of Roses knee. She wailed out in pain. I pushed her off and jumped to my feet.

My hand lifted with my knife gripped in its palm. I could feel False-Ava spell crackling impatiently inside me. *Kill.* It screamed. *Now.* My body shook with its force but I didn't move. I felt dizzy. Nauseous. My mouth began to foam.

Kill. The magic screamed inside me. *Kill.*

Every muscle hurt as I struggled not to move. I would resist. I had to. I would fight the command like Rose said I could.

Kill. Kill. Kill.

Saliva trailed down my chin, dripping like drops of blood onto the stone. My consciousness blurred. Where was I? Who was this beautiful woman standing in front of me, stopping me from doing what I wanted? She had to die. I couldn't remember why but she had to die and I had to kill her.

Yes. I pulled back my knife to strike. I had to kill her.

Rose saw the motion. She saw that I was losing the struggle. She turned and ran.

I leapt after her. My feet pounded against the stones, faster and faster with each step, bounding forward like a lion on the hunt. The pain in my legs didn't matter, nor did the soreness in my side. The ice cold wind biting at my skin. All that mattered was catching Rose.

She ran. I chased. Across the inner ward, through the menagerie of statues. She circled around the animal statues of her ancestors, weaving behind them for cover, but I was too fast to lose track of her. My eyes stayed locked onto the bright red of her cloak as she ran. It beckoned me forward like the red I saw inside.

At last Rose gave up seeking cover behind the statues. She darted past the stables toward the cathedral. The huge stone building loomed before us, smothered in carvings of vines and animals. An opulent wilderness large enough to swallow us both with its majesty. I ran after her with unearthly speed, propelled by False Ava's magic.

I was close now. A few more paces and I could touch Rose's messy red curls. Her cloak fluttered in the darkness of early morning. Pure compulsion moved me forward. My entire being was worn. My limbs weak. My chest burning with the pain of running. I couldn't stop. Another step and I could touch her. I could end this painful dance with a quick slice of my knife.

Rose stopped at the cathedral door. She pushed against the heavy oak but it was locked. I reached out my hand. My fingers tangled into her hair.

A quick gust of wind blew her curls away, biting against my fingers like the slice of a knife. In the same moment Rose began to climb. She lodged her feet into the cracks in the stone wall of the cathedral and moved upward like a star climbing up to the heavens.

I stopped and looked up. My heart pounded like a woodpecker's beak. She was already too high for me to fling my knife. I placed the blade in my mouth and climbed up after her. The iron taste of blood pressed against my tongue as I struggled to climb in my gown. The skirt ripped, creating a slit in the blood-stained velvet. Up and up I went. My arms and thighs burned. I almost slipped twice but I moved forward. Steady. Determined.

Only one thing mattered. Satisfying the magic. Obeying the command. Silencing the voice in my head. *Kill,* it screamed. *Kill. Kill. Kill.* Only then could I rest.

All at once the wall ended. I pulled myself up onto the roof. Rose stood, facing me. A strong wind swept over the cathedral. Her red curls fluttered in front of her face. I saw her shiver beneath her cloak.

I pulled my knife out from between my teeth.

Kill. Kill. Kill.

I needed to silence the screaming. This constant buzzing in my mind.

A sound caressed my ears suddenly. It melted through my whole body. Soft. Light. Warm. A wrinkle appeared in False-Ava's magic as I tried to riddle out what it was.

A song. Rose's song.

How long had it been since I had heard that sound? Not since we had defeated Lucille together. How long ago it was. What children we had been.

Rose's song had comforted me night after night in our cottage when it was I who had been having nightmares. It had kept the ghosts away in the woods the night we had first held hands.

Sweet. Eerie. The magic of her song seeped into me, loosening memories like ripples inside my head. They melted through my veins, infecting every part of me. Rose and I lighting a bonfire together in the woods. Rose, bursting free from the grip of Lucille's magic. Rose, holding me as I slept, chasing the darkness away. Gerti's command crackled angrily against the song but it continued to flow through me. Strong. Warm. Like honey. Like fire. Like melting butter. I remained still, captivated by it's hypnotic lilt.

Kill. The command screamed but I ignored it. Let my flesh rip to pieces if it wanted to. I wouldn't kill what I loved most in the world. I wouldn't kill Rose.

Kill. Kill. Kill.

The spell screamed and screamed, vibrating through me like thunder but I would not listen. I would not hurt Rose. I would stop myself.

I held out my hand, uncurled my fingers, and dropped my knife. It clattered against the roof of the cathedral, echoing into the night.

Rose smiled. "I knew you could do it."

"I love you." I told her.

Kill. The spell screamed again. *Kill Otto and anyone who tries to stop you.*

I had stopped myself.

Kill. Kill. Kill.

I was powerless to resist the command. I had to obey.

Kill Otto and anyone who tries to stop you.

My body moved against my will as I obeyed. I stepped back and let myself fall off the edge of the cathedral.

ROSE

I felt her fall. My song circled inside her. I felt the rush of wind tangle in her hair. I felt her long, white gown ripple around her feet. I felt her heartbeat quicken, beating faster and faster until it stopped altogether. I felt her body go cold and her breathing stop long before she hit the ground with a heavy crack of bones. I felt the snow crunch beneath her.

Dead. No. She couldn't be dead.

The wind wound its way into my hair as I stood on top of the cathedral. My fists clenched at my sides, almost as pale as Snow's complexion. I looked around for a way down. Dawn was just beginning to brighten the sky into a colorless gray. I spun around on the piece of roof I stood on, numbly, until I found a window. It wasn't locked. I crawled through it into the library of chained books Snow had told me about. I sneezed from the dust. There was a door. I followed it down into a long dark staircase, winding down and down until I reached the hall of the cathedral. I moved as if in a dream, hardly aware of what my body was doing. Shadows filled the space inside the massive building as my feet echoed against the stones. I pushed the heavy oak doors open. They were not locked from the inside. A chill swept through the chapel. I shivered and stepped outside.

A blanket of snow glittered across the ward in the early morning sun. Tiny bits of ice, both fragile and deadly. Snow's body lay in the middle of it.

I stopped when I reached her. She lay sprawled across the ground. Her long blood-stained gown was pushed up to her knees, shifted by the wind when she fell. Her black hair fell across her face and neck. I knelt beside her and pushed it away so that I could see her lips, no longer their bright, apple red. They hung open in a stupid, dead expression. The touch of her skin was cold and numb as she stared up at me with unseeing eyes. The last traces of blood had gone from her cheeks.

I placed my forehead against hers, not caring how cold she was. My life would be so hollow without her, as if I were the corpse. I felt my breath flow through my body. My heart beating in my chest.

I cradled her body with my magic, unwilling to let the connection break just yet. My song clung to every broken piece of her. As if that could stop her from stiffening with death. As if I could somehow give her the strength to rise up and walk again.

Or could I?

My magic went still inside her. The remaining traces of her warmth were faint. Only a remnant still clung to her like ice on a windowpane, opaque and fragile to the touch. I followed its trace into her blood, no longer pumping in her veins.

I pulled back suddenly, stung with the crackle of anger and pain. Gerti's spell, still clinging to her blood.

I leaned back in, bracing myself this time against the anger.

What a small piece of her I had ever known. The still depth of her touch. The innocent way her eyes widened when she looked at something she loved. The tight twist of her lips when she practiced her knife throws.

Her horrible cooking that was, every once in a moon, brilliant.

Such a small piece of all that she was. I could never come close to knowing the vastness that was inside her.

The vastness that was gone. I searched the remaining shell of her body for a sign of her memories. Her thoughts. Her joys. Her pain. Her knowledge. Anything that would make her Snow again.

Gertrude's spell crackled at me from inside her blood, mocking my search. It stung like nettles. I lashed back at it then stopped.

That pain. It wasn't Gerti's. It was Snow's. A deep loneliness and guilt harnessed by the spell but not created by it. The two were twisted together like bits of wool bound into the same piece of yarn.

Loneliness. Guilt. How had I not seen them? I had been blinded by the dizzying haze of my own nightmares and hadn't seen her suffering in silence beside me.

She had tried to tell me, I realized. She had tried to tell me she was in pain but I had been angry at her. Angry at her for stealing from my happiness. For not loving the dazzling whir of castle life along with me.

Gently, I caressed the pain still resting in her blood. I hummed softly. Mournfully. Then I felt it. Deep inside the stillness of her blood.

Light. Like the moon. Like a lamp in the darkness. Peaceful. Loving. Like the soft press of her kisses.

Snow.

It was faint but strong. There was still time. I could call her back to me. All I had to do was reach out and grasp her light. I could hold her in my arms again. I could tell her I was sorry for asking her to live where she didn't belong. For not listening. I could sooth away her pain.

If it worked. I had never heard of anyone being brought back from the dead. Would she be the same when she came back? Would she be in pain? Did I dare take that risk?

I reached out and touched her light. Gently. Carefully. Hardly grazing it with my song.

"I love you." I said and let go.

I pulled back, returning my awareness to the ward. My song dissipated around me. I struggled to make sense of the scattered notes as they fluttered in the air. Dawn had finished stretching her colors over the sky. I stood up.

"Why did you do that?"

I turned. It was the false Ava. Gerti. Fire burned in my belly as my song settled back inside me. This was the girl who had taken Snow from me. Who had caused Trouble's death.

She cocked her head curiously. Messy gold curls fell across her shoulder. "Why did you let her go? Don't you want her?"

Want her? Of course I wanted her. "She's not a play thing for me to own." I said.

Gerti blinked at me. I could feel the crackle of her magic in the air, harnessed with anger and pain like she had twisted inside Snow. "You could have saved her. You could have called her back. Your magic is strong enough. I can feel it."

I shook my head. Images of Falada's head on a pole flashed through my mind. His flesh decaying around his consciousness. What if I pulled her back to life twisted and broken, condemning her to the same fate as the dead horse? I shuddered to imagine her lurching through a half life enshrouded in the guilt and loneliness that had been coursing through her her last days. I would not take that risk. Life and death were not play things. Let her rest. My happiness in having her back was not worth her pain.

Gerti rolled her eyes. Her curls shifted across her face in the shadow of the cathedral. "Well if you won't, I will. I still need her."

I felt her magic move but mine was quicker. My song erupted in a long screeching wail, encircling the shadow that tried to escape from Gerti. She crackled trying to reach for Snow. I sang louder, gathering strength with each note.

"Let me save her." Gerti whined. "She's my friend."

Friend? She'd tortured her. Forced her into silence. Commanded her to kill against her will. And now she wanted to disturb the peace of her death. Ava had been her friend and she'd stolen her life from her and condemned her to silence.

"Friends are not things you can own and do with as you please." I said. "They are not puppets. They do not exist for your amusement."

My song strained against her laughter. It wavered, unable to hold back the crackling force of her mirth.

Gerti's magic shot through me, looking for something to latch onto, to twist into its will. My feelings mingled with hers. Pain. Loss. Loneliness. A deep void begging to be filled with anything it found. Life without Snow. Life as a servant. Life alone.

How could I sing with that emptiness inside me?

I closed my eyes, touched the pain, then found my fire. It lit up like a furnace. Flames roared against the insides of my heart, licking away with a renewed vigor. I ripped myself away from her grasp and commanded her to be still.

ROSE

I stood in Otto's throne room next to Ava -the real Ava. The courtiers crowded around, eager to witness their king pass judgement. Grace clutched her hand against her heart, fanning herself with a silk fan. Bastian whispered something in his young lord's ear. Otto rose from his throne. The chatter quieted slowly as everyone waited for him to speak.

"Will Conrad the goose boy please step forward?" He asked.

Conrad stepped out of the crowd. He held his chin up high but I could see his hands shake as he pulled his hat off his head and clutched it in his hands. He bowed.

"Conrad," Otto said, "For the service of telling me of Princess Ava's magic and stirring my curiosity enough that I went to check on her and met her and learned to understand her enough to know when she needed me to stay and listen, I grant you the title of Head Goose Boy. And to compensate for the daily torment you suffered at the hands of my betrothed I grant you access to the services of the royal hat maker for the rest of your life. May you never fear having a bare head again."

Conrad stumbled to his feet. He stared, dumbfounded. "The royal hat maker?" He asked. "Could I get one with a feather in it?"

"Absolutely. As many feathers as you like."

"Could I have more than one hat at the same time?"

"You can have thirty if you so desire."

"Thirty hats." The boy mouthed the words, staring at Otto in amazement. A guard stepped forward and gently tapped him on the shoulder. "Thirty hats." He mouthed again and allowed himself to be led, gently, back into the crowd by the guard.

"Lord Bastian." Otto called next.

Bastian stepped away from his young lord. He wore a red coat with feathers on it. They spread like wings as he bowed low before his king with an exaggerated flourish.

"For confessing to the crime of theft with the intention of smuggling I sentence you to three months of serving Sludge in the kitchen, preparing meals for the castle. It seems only fitting that you aid the person you have caused the most distress. You will find Sludge a very instructive master. You will also return or replace every scrap that was taken. May you, in the future, treat the gifts of my subjects with more respect."

"Yes, my king." Bastian bowed again. This time with more solemnity and less flourish. His coat drooped. He stepped back and joined the other courtiers.

"Gertrude of the Southern Ridges."

I flinched when Otto called out the name. My eyes strayed to the end of the hall as the guards brought her forward. Her wrists were bound with heavy iron chains that had worn dark bruises into her Ivory skin. She trudged forward, stumbling with her head hung down, until she reached the foot of Otto's throne. The guards pulled her to a stop.

"Gertrude." Otto said. "You are charged of the murder of Alf the Forester and Asher the Merchant in addition to causing the deaths of his daughter Mirah, my faithful servant the hobgoblin Trouble, and my very dear friend Princess Snow. I will, however, leave your fate in the hands of she who is still living whom you have harmed the most. My betrothed, Princess Ava, whose life you attempted to steal and who you condemned to silence. Ava, my love, what shall this girl's sentence be?"

Ava stepped forward. It was strange to see her dressed as a courtier in a thick embroidered gown. In place of the braided coil I was accustomed to seeing on top of her head was a simple gold circlet. She looked at Gerti, held still between the two guards.

Gerti's curls were damp and muddy. Her face streaked with dirt from her cell. The bruises on her wrists were almost black. She hung her head, keeping her eyes on the ground almost as if she didn't know Ava and the rest of the court were there at all.

Ava's eyes filled with sorrow. "I am far from the person you have harmed the most with your carelessness, Gerti." She said. "By happy accident I have escaped your blood binding and regained my life but those who loved the lives you took" she glanced up at me and then at Trouble's brothers crowded around Otto's throne in their matching gold coats. "They will never regain what they have lost.

"The secrets of shade magic are guarded very carefully by my family. We use them sparingly and we have a very specific sentence for those of us who abuse that power. It is to be put in a barrel of iron nails and rolled down a mountain. Only the iron can weaken the magic enough so that it cannot be used again, even in death. As a protector of shade magic it is my duty to uphold this punishment unfailingly against those who abuse it, but Gerti, as my friend, I do not wish to see you suffer this fate. Promise me you will never use any magic again and, against my betrothed's wishes, I will grant you absolute mercy. Make that promise and you can live with us forever in our castle."

Gerti's head remained down, hanging like a damp rag as the guards held her still. The entire court remained silent, waiting for her to answer.

"Gerti, please."

Gerti looked up at last. Her eyes flashed. "Don't call me Gerti." She spat. "That is a servant's name. Call me Gertrude."

"Gertrude." Ava amended.

Gertrude laughed. The chains hanging from her wrists rattled against the ground as her body shook. "I will never live in your castle again, Ava. I will not bow to you and call you queen. Throw me in a barrel of nails if you choose. I will promise you nothing."

Ava nodded. "As you choose. I did not choose to be a princess, Gertrude. I never asked to be a queen but I did choose you to be my friend and my companion. I loved you, Gertrude. You were like a sister to me. I would have given you anything if you had only asked."

Gertrude's face darkened with hatred. "I should never have had to ask." She said.

The execution was held that night on top of a cliff just outside the castle. The entire court was welcomed but only Ava and I came. We stood next to Otto and watched as Gertrude was placed in a barrel full of nails and dropped off the cliff. The wind was too loud for us to hear her scream as she fell down onto the rocks. The barrel burst open as it hit the ground. The guards retrieved er body, covered in blood marks from the nails, and we buried her in the village graveyard.

I insisted on preparing Snow's body for burial myself. Touching it felt like touching a snake's skin. Fragile. Empty. Cold. I bathed her and dressed her in fresh linen then laid her in her coffin, crossing her arms gently over her breasts

I ate something. I don't know what it was or who handed it to me but they told me to eat and so I did. I slept too but I don't know when or for how long. I only know that eventually it was day again and I was carrying Snow's coffin back to the cathedral to put in the crypt. The hobgoblins helped me carry her. They had forgiven her for killing their brother. She had been under a blood binding even if she had been able to resist it for me but not for him.

The hobgoblins stood in a circle around her coffin. There were Nimble's long fingers and Sludge's floppy hat. Glen's wide beard and thick eyebrows. Lad's long, gawking face. Quill's ink smudged hands. My gaze fell on each of them as they bore their brother's killer across the ward. It was so strange to see them all gathered together without Trouble. Trouble had been the first to believe in my magic. He'd seen it long before I knew it was there.

Otto placed his arm around me but I felt no comfort in his touch. I walked beside him, barely aware that my body was moving. I turned to look at him. The hurt in his eyes mirrored mine. Water flowed, dribbling salt into my mouth.

A long progression formed behind us. Nimble played a mournful dirge on his pipes. Drummers beat their instruments in time with the pipe as we walked. Lords, ladies and servants alike trailed after us, adorned from head to toe in black. They had come here for a wedding. Were they angry that they were at a burial instead?

No. Not angry. Just sad.

Sad. What a tiny word for all this loss. As if a single syllable could encrypt the pain pounding against my chest like a sledgehammer, absorbing my limbs so that they felt like led.

It was at that moment that I realized I was wearing red instead of black. Had Louisa dressed me in this or had I dressed myself? I couldn't remember but I didn't think Snow would mind. She would have been happy to see me in anything no matter the color. Even for her own funeral.

And red was my color. The color of fire. The color of Roses.

At last we stepped into the cathedral. Snow would have liked the way Nimble's flute echoed in the wide, open space. She would have liked the way light poured through the stained glass and painted rainbows on her pale, still face as we carried her across the chapel.

The crypt was dark and cold. Only Otto, me, and the hobgoblins entered, bearing Snow's body. Snow's name was carved on a stone slab toward the side of the room.

Glen grunted. "We did the engraving. You big folk use your true names in life so it doesn't pull the same weight but we did it just the same."

I glanced at Otto, confused. Trying to make sense of what they were saying through the haze of my grief.

"It's a hobgoblin ceremony." He said. "Their true names are only used on the day of their birth and the day of their death. It's an honor. One Snow is more than worthy of."

Trouble's slab was a few feet away. His tiny coffin was placed on a slab with an engraving of its own. Otto had insisted he be buried in the royal crypt. I should have been curious about what his true name was but I wasn't. He would always be Trouble to me.

We placed Snow's coffin on her slab. I stared down at her unmoving form, trying to memorize the curve of her nose. The shape of her chin. Too quickly they would fade from my mind. Her apple red lips parted in a stupid expression as she stared up at me with unseeing eyes. I tried to think of something beautiful to say. A goodbye that held enough meaning but no words came. Instead I bent my head down and pressed my lips softly against hers. They were cold. Stiff. Still.

My fire stirred inside my breast. It danced and flickered like a harvest bonfire. What a gift knowing her had been.

Made in United States
Troutdale, OR
06/06/2024

20384029R00108